The Treasure Bird

The Treasure Bird

PENI R. GRIFFIN

SILVER BURDETT GINN

Needham, MA   Parsippany, NJ
Atlanta, GA   Deerfield, IL
Irving, TX   Santa Clara, CA

SILVER BURDETT GINN
A Division of Simon & Schuster
160 Gould Street
Needham Heights, MA 02194–2310

Simon & Schuster edition, 1996

4 5 6 7 8 9 10   BA   01 00 99 98

ISBN 0–663–59266–6

To Morgan, Amy, Becky, and Christy,
my stepfamilies

Contents

1/ Letters

"MARLY'S WORKING late again." Daddy sighed as he unlocked the apartment door after bringing Jessy home from the speech therapist. Matt had been by the laundry room playing dodgeball as they drove in, and signs of his return—books on the couch, jacket over a chair back—were scattered all over, but Marly's keys were not on their hook, and the mail waited in an unsorted pile. Daddy sorted it while Jessy poured two glasses of juice. "Here's one from Mommy," he said, holding out a small grayish envelope addressed in familiar handprinting. Jessy seized it and ripped it open, as Daddy added, "It must be about the visit. What does it say?"

The first words she saw were "I'm terribly sorry." Jessy sank into a kitchen chair, eagerness twisting in her stomach and becoming anxiety. She waggled her hand at Daddy to be patient, and read without looking up.

Dear Jessy,

I'm terribly sorry to disappoint you, and I'm disappointed myself, except that I'm also very excited—

She changed communes again, thought Jessy. Maybe she's just putting the visit off a little while.

I couldn't possibly tell you all the amazing things that have been going on here. It's revolutionary! But also terribly sad. You remember I told you about Brother Samuel?

He had been in the picture Mommy had sent with the last letter—a skinny man, more or less handsome if you didn't mind the shaved head and the baggy white clothes people wore in that commune. Mommy called him her mentor, which Daddy had explained was a kind of teacher.

He has received a Great Enlightenment, a Vision that transforms the whole Movement! It is a long hard road ahead, but I feel sure we have our feet on the True Way at last! Sadly, Father Noman—corrupted by worldly pride we fear—has rejected the Revelation and forced a schism—a split in the Community of Faith! So we are setting forth into the wilderness to find a base from which to struggle toward the light.

Okay, thought Jessy, relaxing. So once she gets moved she'll send for me. Maybe Daddy'll be ticked off about having to change the plane tickets, but he'll live.

But—the struggle is even longer and harder than we supposed. Brother Samuel's vision shows this clearly! And the worst of it is, it is hard even on those whose feet are not yet on the beginning of the path! (Huh? thought Jessy.) Such is the sad nature of the world. In order to see it through, it is necessary to abandon all earthly ties—even the dearest, most sacred ones—and do as Jesus and the Buddha and all the Great Leaders have done—devoted themselves to the Universal Spirit and left behind all the Bonds of this fleshly life that tie us to the earth, prevent us from achieving the Great Treasures of the Spirit, and liberating the world from the endless round of sorrow and futile endeavor in which it is caught.

Jessy reread this sentence. It didn't make sense the second time either. Mommy's letters were always like vocabulary exercises, with lots of hard words, but this was worse than usual.

"What's the matter?" asked Daddy.

Jessy waggled her hand at him again. Lately he and Marly had been making her talk instead of using signs, but she didn't have any concentration to spare right now. Her stomach began to ache nervously.

Please believe me, baby, I wish I could have you out here as we planned. I've cried and cried about it but Brother Samuel is <u>ADAMANT.</u>

As well as printing in capitals, Mommy had underlined "adamant" twice. Jessy wondered what it meant. Stubborn, maybe.

His Vision is very clear. It's only as a great favor and because we'd already made the plans that he's letting me write to you. We must cut off all contact with our former lives At Once, and not see or speak or, if we can help it, even think of our family or friends in The World until we have Achieved the Goal. I know you'll understand. It's so hard on both of us, but the Quest is so important—

Jessy crumpled up the paper and scooted back her chair so hard it bumped into the counter, the table skidding forward into Daddy's stomach. "Hey, what's up?" he asked sympathetically.

Jessy threw the letter across the kitchen and tried to shout "I hate her!" but she couldn't get past the first sound. She stormed into her room, slammed the door, and hurled herself onto her unmade bed.

First she cried, then she stood up on the bed and stamped till she couldn't keep her balance any more, then she cried again. When Daddy knocked and asked to come in she threw the stuffed baby harp seal Mommy had sent her for Christmas at the door and screamed, "G-g-g-it!" So he went away, and the world outside her blinds got dark, and Matt and Marly came in. She could hear talking in the living room, voices without words, except once for Matt saying, "Poor kid." She gritted her teeth and dug out a handful of Kleenex to blow her nose.

After awhile the smell of Hamburger Helper crept under her door. She rolled onto her back and stared at the ceiling. She was too big to throw tantrums, but nobody would say so. Matt would even be extra nice. He'd probably offer to let her use his Nintendo or something. He wasn't such hot stuff just because his father was a marine and sent him letters from Kuwait every month. He didn't actually see his dad any more often than Jessy saw Mommy. Only he would now, because what that letter said was that Jessy would never see Mommy again, not until she'd found what she'd gone to the communes to look for.

Jessy's old stuffed tiger, Jump, was tangled in the covers. She pulled her out, looking into the single remaining amber plastic eye. Jump had been brand-new when Mommy left. Jessy could barely remember being four, and hanging onto Jump's thick, plush tail with one hand while Mommy hugged her good-bye. She had made Mommy kiss Jump, too, which was a stupid little-kid thing to do; but then, she'd been a stupid little kid at the time.

She had gone to visit Mommy in her different communes several times before she figured out why Mommy had to leave them. The world was all messed up, with wars, and crime, and like that, because people didn't know the One True Way to live. If Mommy and her friends could find the One True Way, the world would be perfect, and she could come home. All the communes had been different, but everybody in each of them had agreed that there was only One True Way, and that they had the responsibility of finding it for everybody else.

Jessy'd never seen Father Noman's commune. Mommy had sent her that picture, of a bunch of bald people in white robes standing around a signpost that pointed up to heaven, down to hell, and sideways to places like Greed, Drugs, and so on. Mommy had changed her name from Grace to Sister Deborah, and she'd said that this new place would be too rough for Jessy the first year. They'd been all set for this summer, though. As soon as school let out, Jessy was to live for two weeks in a log cabin with Mommy and her roommates, Sister Beulah and Sister Handmaid. There would be goats and chickens, a lake for swimming, and singing every night.

Only Brother Samuel's vision had spoiled it.

Why couldn't Mommy have put off going with Brother Samuel a month? Jessy wondered. What was the big hurry? The One True Way wouldn't get found before June, and even if it did, Brother Samuel could tell Mommy how to get on it when she showed up. Why was starting a new commune so much more important than seeing Jessy?

"Supper," said Matt's voice, as he knocked on the door. Jessy rolled over, into reach of the door, and knocked back to let him know she was coming. Nobody had called her for her turn to set the table, which meant somebody had taken her turn for her, which was nice of somebody, she guessed. She hoped no one expected her to feel better because of it.

She was the last one at the table. Marly was still in her business suit. Daddy wore the apron. Matt had hooked his United States Marine Corps cap onto the back of his chair, and he smiled straight at Jessy over the steaming chili mac. Jessy looked at her plate. She said grace along with them silently, in her head, though lately she'd managed it out loud without much trouble.

The chili mac, rolls, and glazed carrots went around the table. Jessy could see Daddy and Marly looking at each other, and Matt waiting for them to speak. Marly was the first to speak.

"I'm sorry you got such bad news today," she said.

"Yeah, bummer," said Matt.

Jessy shrugged.

"Maybe next year she'll have changed her mind again," said Daddy, picking the beans out of his chili mac, "and she'll pick a commune that allows visitors."

"Anyway, I got some news today, too," said Marly, using her brave, sensible voice. "I don't expect this'll make you feel any better right now, but at least it looks like you won't be stuck around here all summer. You remember last week I got a call that my Great-Uncle Matthew had died?"

Jessy nodded. She'd been surprised at how bad she'd felt about that. Great-Uncle Matthew had been nice to her during that horrible three-day reunion they'd gone to after Daddy and Marly got married last year. It wasn't his fault he was old and ugly. She'd wondered what had happened to his parrot.

"Well, today I got a letter that he'd left us some things. You remember the house, and all that land with the creek on it?"

Jessy nodded, thinking, Of course I do, you think I'm stupid?

"I own it now. He left it to me in his will."

Jessy nearly lost her forkful of chili mac. Marly smiled, as if glad to see her expression. "The house, and all the land from the street back to the creek, everything. I can hardly believe it, with so many other relatives to give it to."

"He knew you'd take care of it, though," said Matt. "Most of the Texas relatives already have houses, so they'd sell it."

"Since he didn't leave us any money to pay taxes and maintain the property, we may sell it, too," said Daddy mildly, using his roll to push carrots onto his fork. "Don't get all excited about moving back to Texas till we know for sure where we are."

"I bet he fixed it somehow," said Matt. "Otherwise, there wouldn't be any point. Besides, he wouldn't've left me the parrot if he didn't expect us to be able to stay there. He must've known we couldn't keep it here."

Jessy stared at Matt, not eating. Great-Uncle Matthew had left him the parrot? But—

"Great-Uncle Matthew was a very old man and had trouble keeping his family straight," said Marly. "There's no telling what he had in mind when he wrote that will. He may've gotten me mixed up with my cousin Darlene."

But Goldie should be *my* parrot, thought Jessy, as Matt looked at his plate, looked at her again, and took a roll. I saw her first. She talked to me.

"I'll let you feed Goldie sometimes if you want to, squirt," said Matt, "and Great-Uncle Matthew left you something, too."

Jessy turned to Marly, using her question face.

"He left you Great-Grandma Minnie's samplers," she said. "You know, those things little girls used to practice sewing with, embroidering mottoes and pictures. I remember them in the spare room when we'd visit. They're very old and interesting"—Marly smiled, pretending that somebody's old sewing practice could be as interesting as a live parrot—"and might even be worth money."

"Anyway," said Daddy, "this opens up all kinds of possibilities. You know Marly's about fed up with her job anyway. We were thinking, once school lets out, she could quit and draw her retirement account, and we could go stay in Great-Uncle Matthew's house for a couple of

8 /

months. That way we could get an idea whether it's practical to take the place over, or if we even want to. If it looks like it'd work out, we'll move and I'll get a new job. If not, we'll come back, and Marly'll get a new job. What do you think, punkin?"

Jessy shrugged. If she couldn't go to the commune she might as well go to San Antonio. It couldn't be any more boring than Wichita. And there would be Goldie, and the cats.

"It'll be better than the apartments," said Matt. "There's supposed to be caves down the creek, and there'll be frogs, and catfish, and the parrot, and lots of cats, and the dog." He turned to Marly. "Could I get a metal detector?"

"No you can not," said Marly firmly. "I'm not going to have you digging up that whole property."

"What do you want a metal detector for?" asked Daddy.

"Oh, Great-Uncle Matthew used to joke about buried treasure on the property," said Marly, taking a drink of milk, "and the cousins all got hold of it, and repeat it like gospel truth. If there was a fortune in gold doubloons out there, Great-Uncle Matthew would've dug them up a long time ago, before he ever sold off anything to developers."

"But there doesn't have to be gold doubloons," said Matt. "People collect old bobwire, and bottle caps, and stuff. There could be a fortune in old junk out there. Enough to pay taxes."

"You'll just have to make our fortune without a metal detector," said Marly. "We're going to be on a tight budget this summer while we figure out what we're going to do." Two little lines formed between her brows as she looked at Daddy—checkbook lines, Matt called them, because they appeared every time she looked into the checkbook. "Quitting my job is a big chance to take—"

"What is life without danger?" asked Daddy breezily. "You hate your job and your boss. We hate hearing you talk about how much you hate your job and your boss. All of us would gladly risk anything to get you out of that job. Right, kids?"

Matt nodded vigorously, his mouth full, and Jessy nodded, too, partly because Daddy wanted her to, and partly because she'd always thought Marly made too much fuss about having a job. Mommy had never had one at all.

Jessy cleaned her plate but didn't go for seconds, listening to the others talk about the trip with part of her head, and wondering about Mommy with the rest. What sort of vision had Brother Samuel had? Maybe God had picked Mommy out specially to do something? No, she'd've mentioned that, first thing. Jessy rinsed her plate and cup, and stuck them in the dishwasher.

"Hey, squirt," said Matt, "you want to play Nintendo after homework?"

Jessy shook her head.

"I know," said Daddy, "let's go out for ice cream."

Jessy knew he wanted to make her feel better, but just because he wanted to didn't mean she'd let him. She shrugged, and went back to her room, knowing they'd call her when they were ready.

2/ Properties

JESSY'S DISAPPOINTMENT had faded to a deep, dull ache by the time school let out for the summer. The morning they got up at the crack of dawn to make the long drive from Wichita to San Antonio, she was even looking forward to the trip. Marly's face was all shiny with gladness to be rid of her job, Matt kept running on about the creek and the parrot and the dog, and Daddy smiled every time he looked at Marly. By the time they got to the San Antonio city limits sign, though, Jessy was tired and restless.

"It's hard to believe how far out the city's grown in the last fifteen years," said Marly, waving one hand at the housing developments, apartments, and office buildings on either side of the highway leading into San Antonio. "They'd begun building out here when I left, but this was mostly big empty spaces."

"There's probably big empty spaces further from the highway," said Daddy.

"But how long will they stay that way? I wouldn't mind so much if the developers put up anything but trash." She jabbed her finger at what looked like a string of garages, painted cream and dark brown. "What is the point of building anything *that* ugly and calling it a business park? How can you call it a park if you don't have one blade of grass?"

Park like in parking lot, thought Jessy. Everything looked okay to her, not much different from Wichita. It wasn't as pretty as a commune, but Mommy said cities were sores on the face of America, anyway, so what could you expect?

Marly drove down a steep exit ramp, turned back under the highway, and the world changed.

Daylight had glared on the highway and the business park, but down here evening was already sneaking in underneath the overpass and the trees. The street was a strip of untidy asphalt laid down on top of the weedy ground. On the left was a rail fence and a big arched gate that said GRASS CREEK STABLES. Jessy stopped slouching against the door and sat up straight. That hadn't been here last year! Marly turned right and stopped so Daddy could open the gate in a chain-link fence. Gravel ground noisily under the tires as they drove slowly up the long driveway to the white garage near the yellowish white stone house. It was just the way Jessy remembered it, a space of regular yard and then nothing but unused land and stubby trees as far as she could see. Yellow roses bloomed over the front porch, where an old lady and a black dog stood up as they stopped the car.

"Welcome home," said Great-Aunt Lucy, coming down the steps to hug Marly. She was not as ugly as Great-Uncle Matthew had been, partly because she was plumper and the wrinkles didn't show as much, but she was about as old, and her blouse and slacks did not fit. The dog kept close to her legs, growling softly. "Hush, Clyde," she said, shoving him with her knee.

"Come on, Clyde, you remember me." Matt put down his suitcase to let the dog smell him, holding him by the collar as Jessy did the same, as if he thought she would be scared. To prove she wasn't, she petted Clyde and scratched him behind the ears, feeling her hands get dirty, but making him wag his tail.

"Y'all come in this house now," said Great-Aunt Lucy, leading them up the steps. "No, leave Clyde; I never have let him in. He's not housetrained or anything. My, you kids have grown such a lot in this year!" The hall seemed dark and crowded, with five people, four suitcases, and too many tables and hatracks and pictures. The smell of roast beef and roses and pine cleanser did not cover up the sour smell strange houses always seemed, to Jessy, to have. "I put you and Tad in the master bedroom down here, Marly. Dinner'll be ready in half an hour. You kids can run around outside till I ring the bell if you want, but I bet you'd like to see your inheritances first."

"Yes, please," said Matt.

"Goldie's out on the screened side porch where Matthew kept her in summer, but I warn you, she's been pretty poorly since he passed on." Great-Aunt Lucy pointed Matt in the right direction and he went. Marly and Dad were already heading for the master bedroom.

Before Jessy could follow Matt, Great-Aunt Lucy turned a polite smile on her. "I fixed my old room for you and put your samplers in there. Can you carry that big old suitcase upstairs all by yourself?" Jessy nodded. It wasn't as big a suitcase as all that! "Come up with me, then, and I'll show you." Working her legs as if they were not attached very well, Great-Aunt Lucy started upstairs, and Jessy had either to follow or to explain that she'd rather see Goldie than her samplers.

"It's getting so I can't hardly get up these stairs anymore," said Great-Aunt Lucy. "Won't be anything to your young feet. Good night! When I think how I used to run up and down when I was a girl, it makes my legs ache! I'm so glad I got that apartment in the block here back of the creek. This is a wonderful house to be a kid in, but you get old, give me a place all on one floor anytime. Not but what it isn't a shame to see that old back pasture built on. We used to own all that land back there, you know. Many's the time I helped bring the cattle home across the ford! Oh, well, people got to live somewhere, I guess."

Jessy had passed her as she was talking and looked in the doors of the two front rooms on either side of the stairs, finding them crowded and dark, but Great-Aunt Lucy puffed down to the second door on the left of the broad hall. "This here's your room. It was my room when I was your age, and I think it's the prettiest one in the house, but it won't hurt my feelings if you want to move. I don't know much what little girls like anymore." She watched Jessy walk in, anxiously, as if it mattered more than she said that Jessy like her old room.

The curtains were open, letting light in and showing a wide stretch of yard, the trees that marked the creek, and the first building or two of the apartment complex. The windows came down close to the floor with sills deep enough to sit on. The wallpaper was green with pink roses. There was a little too much furniture, but it at least was shoved out of the way. Jessy plotted her sentence as she set her suitcase down, "It's very pr-pretty."

"Well, I'm glad you think so," said Great-Aunt Lucy, her wrinkles changing shape as she smiled. "I hung your samplers over your bed, and that quilt is one my mother made, and I embroidered the pillow slip; so that's three generations of needlework. You ever sew or embroider at all?"

Jessy shook her head, politely going to look at the large frame over the brightly quilted bed. Three separate pieces had been framed together. "Seek and ye shall find," ran across the top in letters made of tiny red *x*'s. On the left side more *x*'s, mostly yellow, brown, and green, said, "Talk is silver, silence gold," inside a border of coins and flowers. On the right was a picture, sewed in lots of different colors and stitches, showing a house near a creek, surrounded by fences, sheds, livestock, and people. This one said, "Home Sweet Home."

"That there's a map of the way the farm looked right before Mama got married," said Great-Aunt Lucy. "She worked on it for years. See, she even put in the stepping-stones there at the ford by the corral. And the orchard—that got blighted; all we got now is the pear tree by the garage—and the silo and the garden—and everything." Great-Aunt Lucy's talking wound down. "You don't say much, do you?"

Jessy shook her head and turned around.

Great-Aunt Lucy was looking anxious again. "Cat got your tongue? Or is it just because you stutter? Sorry, they don't say *stutter* anymore, do they? Because of the speech impediment?"

Jessy nodded. She didn't care if anybody said *stutter* instead of *speech impediment*. She was all for short words.

"Tell you what, it don't help any not to talk. The only way to get better is to practice. Why, Matthew used to hardly never talk at all, because of his stutter, but Daddy made him talk and he got lots better after awhile. It didn't all wear off till after he was grown up—matter of fact, it was teaching that parrot to talk cured him, and that wasn't till ten, twenty years ago. But he got along all right."

Great-Uncle Matthew stuttered? Jessy made her question look, but Great-Aunt Lucy didn't notice.

"Wouldn't surprise me none if it was the stutter that made him remember you. Matthew went to a lot of trouble to dig those samplers out of the attic and put them all together in one frame last year. There's about a half a dozen more than I guess are yours, too, but he never did get back to framing those before he—well, I expect you want to go outside, and I got dinner to get, so you go along. Mind you don't go out of sight of the house!"

The last sentence was called after her, as Jessy set off at once to look at Goldie. Her sandals on the stair carpet made a muffled clatter, but she slowed down going through the dining room, remembering that Goldie didn't like loud noises. She could see Matt standing in front of the cage as she came up.

"Aw, Goldie, come on," he was saying. "I'm your owner now. Good girl. Come on." He sounded tired and impatient.

Jessy went around him to look in the cage, and stepped back in dismay. Goldie was huddled at the bottom of her cage, eyes open, but head down. Her bright green and yellow feathers stuck out untidily around bare patches on her breast and wings, while others drifted among the sunflower seeds and droppings in the tray below her feet. Jessy jabbed Matt and glared at him.

"Hey, it's not my fault!" Matt jabbed back, but not hard. "She was like this when I got here. She won't move or make a sound, except—there, see!" He pointed as Goldie, head bobbing nervously, reached under her wing and picked at a feather. "She's plucking them out her ownself. Goldie! No!" As the bright feather came loose, he slapped the cage. Goldie looked up, hunching her wings, and looked down again. "Oh, what's the use?" he said. "Want to come down to the creek with Clyde and me?"

Jessy shook her head, staring at Goldie. This wasn't one bit like the happy, playful bird that had climbed around her cage laughing last year. "Wh-what's wr-rong, G-goldie?" she whispered. The parrot turned her back and picked under her wing.

Not knowing what else to do, Jessy started whistling. Maybe it would sound like parrot sympathy. She whistled "She'll Be Comin' Round the Mountain," "I've Been Working on the Railroad," and the Ninja Turtles theme without Goldie responding, though in time she turned around. Jessy almost cried with frustration.

"Dinner's almost ready. Where's—oh, my gosh!" Marly plunked down beside Jessy. "Poor Goldie!"

Jessy looked at her hopefully, but Marly just bit her lip and looked upset. "I hope we don't have to take her to the vet. Poor thing! Where's Matt?"

Jessy pointed at the door, but Marly waited for her to speak. Marly could be stubborn about that. "The cr-creek," she said.

"Well, you go wash your hands," said Marly. "We're eating in the kitchen. And don't you fret about Goldie. We'll find out what ails her, and we'll fix it."

Jessy washed her hands, but she didn't see how Marly expected her not to fret. She didn't have much appetite for the dinner Great-Aunt Lucy had fixed, though she could tell it was very good; beef, yams, applesauce, biscuits with honey, and sour cream raisin pie for dessert. She was glad when Matt asked, as soon as grace was said, "Great-Aunt Lucy, what's wrong with Goldie?"

"Oh, she's pining, I guess," said Great-Aunt Lucy. "She and Matthew'd been together so long. And I reckon it's partly my fault. I couldn't very well take her along when I moved over the creek there, and it was such a bother coming everyday, so I got Howard's boy Brandon to feed the animals; but he always has been nervous around Goldie, and I don't guess he did much more than change her food bowls. That feather plucking always means a bird's depressed, according to Matthew's parrot book. I hope now she's got company she'll perk up some."

"Shouldn't we take her straight to the vet?" asked Daddy.

"Don't know but what it'll make her worse," said Great-Aunt Lucy. "She hates the car. And the only vet that Matthew ever would take her to charges an arm and a leg."

"I guess I'll give her a day or two to get used to us," said Marly. "Matt, you better find that parrot book and read up."

But it was Jessy who looked for the parrot book after supper, and found it among the boxes of parrot feed, newspapers, and bird toys on the low shelves by the cage. She found the section on feather plucking and brought it to Daddy, who read it aloud. Parrots plucked their feathers because they were bored, frustrated, had a poor diet, or had hot, dry skin. "Now, I bet Brandon hasn't been giving her her fruit," said Great-Aunt Lucy. "It always was a lot of bother, but I guess if she's used to it the change might be bad for her. Matt, go see if there's any fruit in the refrigerator."

There wasn't; but Jessy fetched the snack box they'd had in the car, and found a couple of oranges nobody'd gotten around to eating. Marly wouldn't let her or Matt offer it to Goldie—"She's sick. There's no telling what she'll do. And she's bitten kids before."—but they stood by the dining room door and watched. At first the miserable bird just ignored Marly, but as she kept talking, softly and encouragingly, and held a piece of orange between the bars of the cage, Goldie stretched her neck toward the bars, and took a chunk. She only ate about half, dropping the rest; but then she took another, and another, until the whole orange was gone. Meanwhile Daddy checked her seed bowl, which turned out to contain mostly dry husks, and refilled it. "I bet Brandon didn't notice she was dropping the husks back in," said Daddy. "I bet he saw it was still half full of something, and never gave her any more."

"I'll tell him a thing or two when I see him," said Matt darkly.

"Let's leave her alone now," said Marly. "We don't want her getting excited. We can keep an eye on her from the living room."

Jessy didn't think this was a good idea. If Goldie was

lonely, she wouldn't want to be left alone again so soon. So Jessy curled up in the armchair nearest to the porch screen door, and watched Goldie sit in her cage with her head under her poor plucked wing.

3/ Treasure

THE SCENT of roses and the sound of birds settling down for the evening came in through the open windows. Great-Aunt Lucy turned on a table lamp, making everything outside the living room seem two shades darker. "It's a weight off my mind to have you here," she said. "You might want to put up some fence at the creek. Ever since people started moving in at the apartments, we've had kids running all over the property."

"Why don't we wait and see if we can afford to stay before we start planning fences?" Marly smiled.

"You know, I've been figuring," said Great-Aunt Lucy. "If y'all need help paying the taxes, I—maybe I can—"

"No," said Marly. "Great-Uncle Matthew left you the money so you'd be able to live without having to worry."

"And don't you think I'd worry if you had to sell off the old place?" Great-Aunt Lucy opened a bag in her lap and took out a half-made lace collar. "The man that built the apartments bugged Matthew to sell. He wants to build a companion complex, he says. But Matthew swore he'd die a pauper before he sold off this one last piece. He must've thought there was some way to pay taxes and upkeep."

"The treasure," said Matt, checking out the cabinets full of knives and china figures and pictures along one wall.

"There isn't any treasure, Matt," said Marly.

"I'm not sure about that," said Great-Aunt Lucy, twisting white thread around a slender metal hook. "Those last few years he'd talk about that robbery every single time the nieces and nephews came over. He'd say there were all kinds of reasons why a thief might not want to spend the money all at once."

"What robbery?" asked Matt. "Wasn't it a miser that buried all his money in a mason jar?"

"Good night! Didn't anybody tell you that whole story?" Great-Aunt Lucy looked accusingly at Marly, who shrugged.

"It never came up."

Great-Aunt Lucy's hands moved, more quickly than Jessy would have thought she could move, and lace appeared magically between them. "See, Matt, this place started out as two farms. My grandad Houston and his brother Lamar took neighboring land—good night, a hundred years ago!" She looked at Matt. "I bet you can't tell me who those brothers were named after."

"General Sam Houston," said Matt promptly, "and . . . um . . ."

"Mirabeau B. Lamar," said Marly. "Presidents of the Republic. Be fair, Aunt Lucy. They don't teach Texas history in Kansas."

"They don't even teach Kansas history in Kansas," said Daddy.

Marly looked shocked. "They don't? Whyever not?"

Jessy fidgeted. Why couldn't grown-ups stick to the point?

"What about the treasure?" asked Matt.

"That was Lamar's. Oh, he was a skinflint! It used to confuse us kids at school, because in history, it was President Lamar that spent money like water, and Houston that tried to pinch the pennies; but in our family, it was the opposite. Grandaddy Houston married him a pretty wife, and gave parties, and was always willing to help out a neighbor. Uncle Lamar never would court the girls because he said they were a waste of time and money, and he patched his clothes till they wouldn't take a stitch anymore. What he didn't raise on his farm, he wouldn't eat. Nobody ever got a present out of him, or a loan, but if he could finagle somebody out of something, he'd do it. Every penny he ever got, he saved it up. He didn't like paper money one bit—wouldn't have it in the house—and silver and copper didn't draw him, either, but he loved those gold coins."

"You mean, you used to carry gold around in your pockets?" asked Matt. "Like quarters?"

"Oh, my, yes; right up to the time Franklin D. Roosevelt put us on the paper money for good. I remember my daddy paying the mortgage man in gold. The coins were all shiny yellow, with stars around the edges, and eagles, and ladies' heads. You could get them from dollar size all the way up to twenty dollars, which was a lot of money in those days."

"A dollar's worth of gold wouldn't come out very big," said Daddy. "That would be, what, a three-hundredth of an ounce?"

"Not in those days." Great-Aunt Lucy shook her head. "Then, gold made the dollars, but now dollars make the gold! I don't like to think what a twenty-dollar piece would be worth now."

"So if we found where old Lamar hid all his money, we'd be filthy rich!" said Matt eagerly.

"I expect you would, if it was on this land," nodded Great-Aunt Lucy. "It wouldn't do you a bit of good to find it over the creek. But I've got my story out of shape now. Where was I?"

"Lamar collected all these gold coins," Matt prompted.

"That's right. Well, my mama was the only child that lived to grow up, and when she was eighteen, Grandaddy Houston had to go over to Austin on business, so he took his wife to see the capitol building. He would've taken Mama, too, but she'd just got engaged and didn't want to go. It turned out to be a good thing, because the train went off the track and a bunch of folks got killed, including Grandaddy and Grandma. As soon as he heard the news, Uncle Lamar was over here trying to take over the property and manage it for Mama; but she wasn't having any of that. The way the will read, or the law went, or something, if she was married Lamar couldn't touch a thing, so she married Daddy the same day as the funeral. Lamar said it was a scandal, but everybody knew he'd dress her in tow sacks, so the neighbors were on her side."

Jessy kicked off her sandals and shifted in the chair, watching Goldie. The parrot shuffled around her cage, one eye glinting amber in the lamplight.

"Grandaddy hadn't left them much to start housekeeping with, and there's always more hard times than soft times for a farmer. But they muddled along best they could, and we got ourselves born—Matthew, and Marly's grandaddy, Mark, and me, and John. It bothered Daddy to be on bad terms with his only in-law, so he patched things up with Lamar best he could, but it wasn't very well. I don't ever recall seeing the inside of his house. Anyway, there were two things bothered Daddy about Lamar's money. One was, that he never would loan any to Mama. He didn't see how anybody could refuse to help his own blood kin; and it was all going to be Mama's anyhow, when Lamar died. The other thing was, he kept it in a gallon mason jar under his porch. Not even in a fence-post bank—just under the porch!"

"What's a fence-post bank?" asked Matt.

"That's where you pulled up a post of your bobwire fence and put your money in the hole. Lamar's back wasn't so good, and I guess pulling that post in and out was too much work. But Daddy kept telling Lamar he'd get robbed; and sure enough, he did!"

"Serves him right, too," said Marly. "That was when Great-Grandad was late on the mortgage payments, and stood to lose everything."

"That's right." Great-Aunt Lucy nodded. "It was the very day Daddy went over to ask him one last time to please make them the loan. 'You don't want to see your own niece turned out of the house your brother built?' he asked. 'Not when a tiny part of this fortune under your feet'—Lamar was standing on the porch—'this fortune under your feet could save her.' But old Lamar said Mama'd made her bed and would have to lie in it. Matthew was along, too, about your age, Matt, and he was so mad he shouted, 'I hope somebody steals every bit of your precious money!' " She looked meaningfully at Matt. "Let that teach you to mind what you say. You can imagine how awful Matthew felt the next day when he found out somebody'd stolen the jar!"

"That can't've been easy," said Daddy. "A gallon jar of gold'd weigh an awful lot."

"It sure would." Great-Aunt Lucy nodded. "That's why us kids never could settle it in our own minds that it wasn't still around somewhere. There weren't any wagon tracks, and that thing'd break your arms if you carried it far. Plus, it had to be somebody that knew where to look. If he'd done any stumbling around in the dark, Lamar would've heard him. The sheriff said they'd catch the thief when he tried to deposit all that money in a bank, or went on a spending spree; but nobody ever did. So we figured he'd hid it nearby, and would go back for it when folks'd had a chance to forget about it."

"Maybe Lamar hid it himself and faked the robbery, so your dad'd stop hitting on him for loans," suggested Daddy.

"That might be," nodded Great-Aunt Lucy. "In fact, Mark and I thought of that. After the house burned down, we searched the rubble. Matthew told us we were wasting our time. Matthew didn't believe in the treasure, in those days."

"I wonder what changed his mind," said Marly.

"Why did the house burn down?" asked Matt.

"I expect Lamar was smoking in bed." Great-Aunt Lucy's hands stopped moving, and she blinked. "He was probably dead from smoke inhalation before we ever saw the fire. When I think—!"

Marly leaned over the table between Great-Aunt

Lucy's chair and the couch and patted her arm. "It was a long time ago. And isn't it something, to know what kind of man your daddy was? Lots of people would've just let the old guy burn."

"Is this something else I don't know about?" asked Matt.

"I must've told you about the fire," protested Marly. "That's how your great-great-grandfather died, trying to save Lamar when his house burned down. Till they tore it up for the apartments, you could still see the chimney and foundation stones in the pasture. The cows liked to graze there because the ashes had made the soil rich."

"I wish it were still there," said Matt. "It'd be worth going to see if y'all missed anything."

"No, it wouldn't," said Marly. "Every child who ever stayed overnight has been over that ruin with a fine-tooth comb. You wouldn't find anything we didn't."

Matt looked disappointed, then brightened. "Something made Great-Uncle Matthew change his mind about whether there was a treasure or not. I bet he figured out where it was and left us clues and things."

This sounded hopeful to Jessy, but Daddy shook his head. "Why not tell us straight out?"

"Because . . . Well . . . Maybe he wanted us to have to work for it," said Matt. "So we'd appreciate it more. Like Mom not helping me with my homework."

"It's a true thing, unearned money never did anyone any good." Great-Aunt Lucy nodded.

Daddy got up and walked over to the cabinets. "You know, I bet it's simpler than that. Marly, how old is this whatnot?"

Marly shrugged. "Who knows?"

"That was Mama's wedding present," said Great-Aunt Lucy.

"Have you already taken all the furniture you need, ma'am?"

"Pretty near. There were a couple of pieces I wanted help with."

Daddy turned around, smiling all over his face. "And nobody else gets to take more than one piece, right?"

"That's right," said Great-Aunt Lucy. "They all took 'em, already. Everything in this house is yours."

"I don't think we need any treasure," said Daddy. "Antiques can fetch a pretty penny."

Marly looked at him as if he were the smartest man in the world.

"I'd rather find gold," said Matt, "but that could keep us going till we find some."

"If there's enough of the right stuff," said Marly, jumping to her feet. "Let's go see!"

Marly, who was an interior designer and knew a lot about furniture, was pleased with the results of the tour. Some of the furniture was a hundred years old, like the brass bed in the downstairs bedroom, and some was modern and trashy, like the recliner on the screened porch, but there was a lot of it—and not just furniture, but dishes and books and ornaments and pictures.

"We'll have to catalog and appraise everything," Marly said as they came out of Matt's room at the front of the house—his grandfather's old room. She turned to Daddy with bright eyes and twisted her hands together. "Oh, Tad! It wasn't real before, but—I really own all this, don't I?"

She said it as if it were the most wonderful, most

important thing in the world. Jessy felt nervous. Daddy took hold of Marly's hands and smiled. "Of course it is. And you're going to keep on owning it."

After Great-Aunt Lucy left, Jessy put her shirts and shorts away in a white dresser, laid Jump on her pillow, and hung her sundresses in a white wardrobe—the bedrooms had no closets, so everybody had a separate piece of furniture to hang their clothes in. Jessy thought that was kind of neat.

The bathroom was kind of neat, too, but it made her feel sad. The bathtub was like the one at Mommy's last commune before Father Noman's, with high curvy sides and lion's feet, and a shower curtain all the way around. Jessy ran a bubble bath, but the longer she sat in the tub the worse she felt.

Marly really loved this house. What if—?

Goldie looked awful, and Matt hardly cared. What if—?

She had written Mommy a letter to let her know where they'd be and that it was okay—which was a lie—about not visiting this year. Daddy said not to expect an answer, and so far there hadn't been one. What if—?

Jessy got out of the tub before she could think of any more *what if*'s, and let the water gurgle away.

Marly was sitting on one of Jessy's wide windowsills with a book in her lap, looking out at the apartments. Pale floodlights shone up the walls, their beams fading as they rose higher, and the yellow windows were squares of solider light. "Hi." She smiled. "How do you like it so far?"

Jessy nodded; then, to keep Marly from telling her to talk, said: "Ok-kay."

"It's too bad about Goldie. We'll get her fixed up soon."

"Okay."

Marly stood up. "May I borrow this book?"

It's your book, thought Jessy. You own everything in the house. But she said, "Okay."

"Thank you. It's one of Aunt Lucy's and Great-Grandma's old bound magazines, really." She held it out for Jessy to see. It had a thick, worn cover with *St. Nicholas* in scrolly letters. "I used to love these when I was your age, and I wanted to see if they were still any good."

"Okay," said Jessy.

"Jessy, what's the matter?" asked Marly.

"N-nothing." Anyway, nothing she felt able to talk about. If she couldn't make the words inside her head, how could she make them in her mouth?

"All right. If you're sure. There's still half an hour till bedtime, so do whatever you want."

Jessy went to the screen porch and sat with Goldie. The parrot looked up when she came in, and hopped toward her. Jessy put her face near the bars, trying not to stutter. "Hello. P-poor G-goldie. G-goldie is a pr-pretty bird." Matt had the TV on in the living room, and it was easier to talk right, knowing that the noise covered the sound of her efforts. Goldie bit the bars gently, climbed up and down the cage walls, and preened her wings, but Jessy kept talking and Goldie kept silent, till Jessy got sick of it. "P-please, talk," she said. "G-goldie, t-talk! T-talk, G-g-goldie, pl-please!"

The parrot paused in the middle of climbing her cage and put her head on one side. "Talk is gold," she said.

If Jessy had not been so used to silence she would have squealed. "G-good g-girl," she said as the TV went dead.

"Talk is gold," said Goldie. "Poor bird."

"Hey, she's talking!" said Matt.

"Shh!" Jessy whirled around, but Goldie had already resumed her climb and no amount of coaxing would start her up again.

"She talked, though," Matt assured Daddy and Marly, as he covered her cage for the night. "I heard her. Had she been talking in here all the time, squirt?"

Jessy shook her head, triumph fighting with resentment. Why did Matt always have to come along and spoil things? "I k-kept t-talking till sh-she ans-ans-answered."

"Good job," said Marly, as Daddy ruffled her hair. "But it's bedtime now. You can go to work on her again in the morning." She kissed Matt and Jessy both, as she had every night since the wedding, and Daddy kissed Jessy but not Matt.

At the top of the stairs, Matt said, slowly, "That was good. I guess nobody told her she was my parrot, not yours."

Jessy nodded.

He took a deep breath and looked over her head. "Anyway, I bet he expected me to share. I bet he only left her to me because I was older. So she can be yours and mine, if you want."

He didn't sound exactly like he did when he was working at being nice to her. Unsure of what to think, she just nodded.

"Okay, then. Good night, squirt." He went to his room, and she went to hers, where she lay on her back under the samplers, on top of the quilt, with the warm air from the open windows blowing over her. All the things that had bothered her earlier were still in her head, but Goldie had talked for her, and the thought of that crowded out the rest until she fell asleep.

4/
Goldie

AS FAR BACK as Jessy could remember she had slept late through the summer, sometimes lying in bed till almost eleven, hearing Daddy moving around, doing housework or whatever.

That had changed when Daddy and Marly got married. This was partly because Marly had a year-round job, so she got up at six o'clock regardless; and partly because she believed breakfast was the most important meal of the day. By seven o'clock, no matter what the day of the week or the month of the year, the apartment smelled like coffee, the radio played bright morning music, and Marly expected everyone to be sitting around the table. At first this had been enough to make Jessy wish Daddy hadn't married her. By now, though, it was hard to sleep past a quarter till seven.

The first morning in Marly's new house, Jessy went to the open window as soon as she woke at six-thirty. The air was heavy and warm, and under the conversations the birds were holding, she could hear the faint sound of the highway. Across the creek, lights were on in some of the apartments—though the sun lit Jessy's room, the apartment windows were all high, small, and curtained—and a few cars were already leaving the parking lot. Jessy smelled roses, and grass, and pancakes. Below her, Clyde and a group of cats waited by the back porch. A screen door banged, and she saw the back of Daddy's bathrobe. "What, you all get breakfast?" he asked them. "Marly! Where's the cat food?"

Jessy went downstairs in her nightgown and pulled the cover off Goldie's cage. The parrot sat on her branch with her head under her wing. "H-hello, G-goldie," said Jessy. "W-wake up."

Goldie didn't stir, but Daddy must've heard her come down, because he came into the dining room and called, "Good morning, punkin! Breakfast's ready."

Jessy looked from him to the parrot cage. She hardly ever had to talk to Daddy. He knew what all her signs and looks meant as well as she did; and sure enough, he understood now.

"Let her wake up on her own. Maybe Matt will let you feed her after breakfast." They heard Matt clumping heavily down the stairs, and Marly singing in the kitchen:

"There's no place like ho-ome!
There's no-o place like home!"

All the windows in the bright, hot kitchen were open, the yellow curtains sucked against the screens by the movement of air. Through the back door Jessy could see Clyde and the cats lined up at a variety of chipped dishes, eating dry food. The wooden kitchen table had been covered by a red-and-white checked tablecloth and was crowded with syrup bottles, milk and juice and coffee, and green glass plates. Marly was lifting the last pancake from a griddle built into the stove top as Jessy took her seat.

"Morning!" said Marly, happily. "We're eating off Depression glass this morning. It used to come free in soap boxes and now people in antique stores pay through the nose for it."

"Shouldn't we save it to sell, then?" asked Matt, helping himself to bacon. He had taken the time to dress, except for his socks and his USMC cap.

"Eating off it won't devalue it," said Daddy, helping himself to four pancakes. "What shall we do today, honey? Catalog everything and decide what we want to keep?"

"That's more than a one-day job," said Marly. She was wearing a leaf green sundress, and her face was pink from the heat. Jessy took two pancakes and passed the platter. She could tell what Daddy was thinking, and she agreed with him; Marly was prettier here than she was at home. She even sounded different, as if being happy was less work here. "We'd better get started, though. I'll want you kids to look over the stuff, too, so we don't go selling anything you want to keep."

"Aw, Mom," said Matt, "I wanted to go exploring today."

"Who says you can't?" asked Daddy. "Just so you put in your claims before we sell anything."

"Exploring where?" asked Marly.

"The creek and the old pastures. I won't go off the property."

"Okay, but you better take Clyde, and my police whistle. There used to be places along the creek where a boy could break his neck." She finished pouring syrup on her pancakes and turned to Jessy. "What are you going to do today?"

"T-talk to G-goldie," said Jessy.

Once the dishes were done and Jessy had dressed, she and Matt took Goldie her breakfast. Goldie stopped worrying at the feathers on her breast, and came toward the bars. Matt talked to her as he took out the water and food bowls and passed them to Jessy to be emptied and refilled. "Hi, Goldie. How you feeling? You going to talk today?"

"Poor bird," said Goldie, watching the dishes. "Chow time."

"Good girl. You talk real good."

"Talk is gold," agreed Goldie, putting her beak in the water dish even before Matt had it all the way back through the bars.

That's wrong, thought Jessy, remembering her sampler. Silence is gold, and talk is only silver.

"I don't think that Brandon ever bothered to clean her cage right," said Matt. Jessy could feel him looking at her, trying to think of a way to get her to do it instead of him. She made herself busy picking out the empty husks from the whole seed in the food dish. He was bigger, and boys didn't gross out as easily as girls did, and anyway, Great-Uncle Matthew had given him the parrot, not her. Matt must have thought of all these things, too, or figured out that he couldn't make her do it, because he made a face and slid the tray out from under the cage. It was pretty icky, but fortunately the ickiest part was all newspaper.

Jessy hooked the seed tray onto the bars, spilling a few on the floor. "Goody-goody! Chow time!" cheered Goldie, as Jessy tore up the last orange to put in her fruit bowl.

Clyde put his paws on the screen door and wagged his tail. "Coming, boy," said Matt, pulling his cap out of his pocket and checking around his neck for the police whistle. "Don't take her out of the cage, okay, squirt?" He left, almost banging the back door, but catching himself in time.

Great-Uncle Matthew took her out, thought Jessy. I bet it'd be a real good idea to take her out. But her beak and claws looked as big now as they had last year, maybe bigger, as Goldie squirted orange juice all over the clean newspaper. Jessy poked in the shelves to see what Great-Uncle Matthew had in his parrot things. There was a spare perch, jingle bells on leather straps, twigs with the bark still on them, and some rawhide dog toys. When she heard the bells, Goldie stopped eating and clapped her wings, making a surprisingly good jingling noise herself. Jessy tied some to the top of the cage, pushing them inside.

Goldie was much better today, jingling her bells, dancing around the cage, and saying silly things at the least encouragement. Not all of the phrases came out right, as if lack of practice had left her rusty. "Talk is Goldie! Gag 'em giggies! Hello! Banktime!"

" 'B-banktime'?" Jessy laughed.

Goldie spread her wings and balanced on her perch. "Ghost bank! Banktime! Batime!"

The noise attracted Daddy and Marly, who had begun to inventory the kitchen. "I bet she's trying to say bath-time," said Daddy. "In that book last night it said they're supposed to get baths regularly in hot weather."

"This isn't hot," said Marly. "You wait till July. But it might not be a bad idea to give her a bath this afternoon."

"And-d 'G-gag 'em gi-gi-giggies'?" asked Jessy, so interested that she forgot what a hard phrase it would be for her till she was already too far in to stop.

"That'll mean 'Gig 'em Aggies,' " said Marly. "Great-Uncle Matthew was a big Aggies fan. That's a college, and 'Gig 'em' is what you yell at their football team." She made a thumbs-up gesture. Goldie cried, "Gigem Gaggies!" and rang the bells.

They all laughed so hard at this Jessy forgot to ask about "Ghost bank."

When Marly went to start lunch, Daddy suggested that Goldie had probably had enough excitement for one morning, so Jessy went around to the back porch to see if the cats were still there. Sure enough, a couple of half-grown kittens stiffened all over and dived for cover when they saw her coming. By the time Marly came out to ring the bell to bring Matt home, they were playing as if they'd known Jessy all their lives. They ran under the house as soon as the bell rang, but Marly assured Jessy they'd come back. "That's another expense," she said, as they went in. "Those cats should be fixed, so we don't contribute to the animal overpopulation problem."

Jessy put shredded cheese on top of her chili. "C-c-can we have s-some ind-d-doors?"

"I don't see why not," said Daddy.

"You know, we're talking like it's settled," said Marly.

"It is settled," said Daddy. "This house is important to you. We'll keep it somehow."

"Four people, a parrot, a dog, and an infinite number of cats cannot live on air. We may not be able—" Marly was interrupted by the thumping of feet on the back porch; not one set of feet, but two, plus Clyde's claws.

Matt burst in, followed by another boy, black and about Matt's age. Clyde almost came, too, but Matt shoved him out again. "Cripes, give a guy time to get here, wouldya?" said Matt, when he saw the others sitting around the table. "This is Curtis. Can he stay to lunch?"

Marly had cooked plenty of chili, and there were chips and canned pears, too, so Curtis and Matt thundered into the downstairs bathroom to wash, and thundered back again. "This is my mom," said Matt, while they pulled up chairs to the bowls Marly had filled for them. "And this is my stepdad, Tad."

"Tad-the-Dad?" said Curtis, smiling a self-contained smile, and shaking hands.

Daddy smiled back. Matt snorted cheerfully. "Tad-the-Dad! That's a good one. And that's my stepsister Jessy."

"Hello, Jessy," said Curtis.

Jessy looked up and nodded.

"She don't talk much," said Matt, rattling the chip bag.

"I think she can manage a hello," said Daddy.

Jessy gave him a dirty look. Daddy looked back at her, steadily. She spoke quickly to show him what a bad idea it was, "H-h-h-hel-l-lo."

"Jeez, squirt, you can do better than that," said Matt. "Pass the cheese, please. Curtis lives over in the apartments, y'all. He was Great-Uncle Matthew's paperboy, and he believes in the treasure, too."

"I don't know why I wouldn't believe in it," said Curtis. "Mr. Holz liked to talk about it."

"Really?" asked Daddy. "What did he say?"

Curtis shrugged. "Oh, he hinted around. He knew I was from the apartments, so he made sure I knew he used to own the land there and that a miser owned it before that. So we used to talk about that. And one day, his sister was having trouble finding the money for the subscription, and he said, 'If she knew I was letting her scrape around after change knowing what I know, she'd kill me.' So I said, 'What is it you know?' And he laughed and said he was a rich man trying to sneak into heaven. But another time, I was fooling with that parrot, getting her to talk, and he asked me, what did I think of when I thought of parrots? So I said, '*Treasure Island.*' And he laughed and said that was exactly right." Curtis let his spoonful of chili drip. "There was a lot of stuff like that. So I figure, he must've known where that miser hid his money, all right."

"Then why didn't he ever dig it up?" asked Daddy.

Curtis shrugged. "Maybe he didn't need it."

"If I knew where there was a treasure in gold coins that was rightfully mine, I'd dig it up before I ever started selling off my land," said Marly.

"Oh, but, hey!" exclaimed Matt. "Maybe he didn't feel like it was rightfully his! You remember how in the story he wished Lamar'd get robbed, and he was? Maybe he got a complex about it and felt like he didn't deserve the treasure, so he left a bunch of clues, or a map, or something for us to find!"

Marly laughed and shook her head. "I don't think that's real likely, hon. Honestly, I think he was teasing everybody. Maybe he even figured if we believed in the treasure we'd hold onto the property longer, work harder to keep it in the family. But I'll have to see this treasure before I believe in it."

"What if I brought it to you?" asked Curtis. "Figured out where it was, and set it in front of you? 'Cause I think I can. I've been studying on it, and I just bet I can."

"Well, if you do, you'll deserve a share," said Marly.

"How big a share?" pressed Curtis. "Will you give me half of whatever I find?"

"Wait a minute," said Matt, "nobody's going treasure hunting on this property without me."

"Okay, a quarter then." Curtis shrugged. "It's still bound to be a lot of money. What do you say? I'll want it in writing."

"Oh, okay," said Marly, "but that won't be the only thing in writing. I don't want this place turned into a strip mine."

So Matt turned to a new page of the legal pad Daddy and Marly had been doing the inventory on, and wrote out what he and Curtis were allowed to do in pursuit of the treasure, and who was entitled to what shares. Once this was stuck on the side of the fridge, Curtis helped Jessy and Matt do the dishes, and then both boys headed for the creek, Clyde bouncing around them.

Jessy considered going to the stable to look at the horses, but it was so hot she chose to go out for groceries with Daddy, instead, because the car and the store would be air-conditioned. They bought carrots with long green tops, peaches and apples and bananas, meat, milk, and lemonade mix. Daddy shook his head over the bill. "We'll have to be nitpicky about spending money. Turn off lights, not buy candy, all that kind of thing."

Jessy nodded.

Daddy looked around before he left the parking lot, trying to remember where he'd left the highway. "We've got to make this work," he said. "There wouldn't be any question of Marly not moving back, if it were just her and Matt; but four people is a lot to feed and clothe."

And send to speech therapy during the school year, thought Jessy.

"I'm going to call all the schools, see if anybody needs an art teacher," Daddy went on, pulling out of the parking lot. "Or any kind of teacher. This house is so important to Marly."

The way communes were important to Mommy, thought Jessy, and felt cold.

5/Sale

MARLY'S COUSIN Rachel, in the antique business, helped with the inventory, wandering around the house with a legal pad, and saying things like, "It's a lovely example of American primitive, but we can't get top price with all that paint on it." Daddy set up a workshop in the garage where he and Marly's cousin Bob stripped paint, sanded, and varnished. Sometimes Matt and Curtis or some of the other cousins helped out.

Jessy enjoyed doing inventory. Marly and Rachel would give her a legal pad and go through the furniture, calling out descriptions, which she wrote down neatly. Marly and Rachel talked about what they used to do when they were little, and sometimes when they got dust in their throats they would all break for cookies and iced tea on the front porch.

Now that she had proper food, company, and a bath from a spray bottle everyday, Goldie had stopped picking out her feathers, but she still didn't talk much. Jessy was certain she didn't get out of her cage often enough, but Daddy and Marly wouldn't let Matt and Jessy take her out themselves. Once when Jessy did it behind their backs, one of the cousins helping with the refinishing came along, tried to play with Goldie, and got bitten. He yelled, Jessy tried to say it was his own fault but was too mad to get the words out, Goldie bent a wing feather and almost escaped out the screen door, the cousin's father got mad at Daddy, which got Marly mad at him, Matt was mad at everybody, and Goldie sat at the bottom of her cage, screaming, "Matthew! Matthew!" It was so awful Jessy sat in the recliner and cried.

She didn't have much appetite that night at dinner. Matt was still mad. "You knew you weren't supposed to take her out," he said. "It would've served you right if you got bit."

"Sh-sh-she w-wouldn't b-bite m-me," said Jessy, hating the way her voice wobbled around. "It-t-t was th-that b-boy's f-fault." She swallowed, trying to slow down. "Gr-great-Uncle Matthew t-took her out every-d-day."

"I think enough's been said on this subject," said Daddy, looking at each of them in turn, sternly. "Jessy'll know better next time, won't you?"

Jessy nodded. Next time, she'd make sure there weren't any stupid boys around!

"But she keeps doing stuff like that," protested Matt. "It's my bird, and she acts like it's hers."

"You d-don't p-pay any attention to her," said Jessy. "You're always out looking for tr-treasure."

"I'm always out working to make sure I can keep her," said Matt. "You think we'd be able to keep a parrot in that puny apartment? If we sell the house, we'll have to sell Goldie, too."

Jessy glared at him.

"That's enough," said Daddy. "Making Jessy feel bad won't help."

"Okay, Tad-the-Dad," said Matt, helping himself to more rice. Marly started talking about a cousin of hers who worked for the school district, who had told her about a school in a nearby small town that needed a wood shop teacher. Daddy made a joke about the number of cousins she had. Jessy picked at her food till the barbecue sauce congealed on the ribs, then excused herself and went to look at her box of samplers.

They had found the samplers in the garage, where Great-Uncle Matthew must have had them while he framed the three now in Jessy's room. She flipped through the box, trying to decide if she liked any well enough to keep. Rachel had said she knew somebody who'd pay up to twenty dollars each for them, so probably not. Maybe she should sell the ones in her bedroom, too?

After a while Marly came in. They could hear the water running and Matt and Daddy talking while they did the dishes. Marly took out a sampler with kittens, puppies, and birds around the edges and the hymn about all creatures great and small in the middle. "I never could figure Great-Uncle Matthew," she said. "Anybody else in the world would have picked this one for a little girl's room before the 'Silence gold' one."

Jessy shrugged.

"We aren't going to sell Goldie, you know," said Marly. "Your dad and I have talked about it. Even if we go back to Wichita, we'll rent a house and bring her with us. Maybe a cat, too. It's past time you kids had some pets."

"A h-house like this?" asked Jessy.

"It would have to be smaller." Marly smiled bravely. "Even a duplex would be better than that apartment, wouldn't it?"

Jessy nodded, thinking, It wouldn't be as good as here. I bet Goldie wouldn't like it. And one cat wouldn't be as good as a half-dozen; and what would happen to Clyde?

Matt didn't say any more about the attention Jessy paid Goldie; but he did start spending an hour a day after breakfast trying to teach the parrot to say "Matt" instead of "Matthew."

The last week of June, a moving van hauled the furniture out to an auction house on the edge of town. It felt strange to walk around the warehouse, finding familiar things tagged and plunked down in the middle of a bunch of strange tables, china cabinets, ornaments, and chairs, as if they were any old stuff out of an antique store. Some old toys, rocking chairs and bicycles and dollhouses, made Jessy hope they would make enough money to bid on a few things themselves; but the actual bidding was boring. The hall was hot and stuffy, the auctioneer talked so fast Jessy couldn't understand a word, and she didn't dare fidget or scratch her nose for fear he would mistake it for a signal that she wanted to buy something. Finally, Marly gave Matt some quarters and sent them to get Cokes and sit outside.

A bald-headed man had decided to do the same thing. He sat on the cement step and stretched his legs out toward the grass, with a can of Dr Pepper sweating in his hand. He smiled unconvincingly. "Pretty boring if you're not buying or selling, isn't it?" he said.

"We *are* selling," said Matt, "but our stuff isn't up yet."

"It's not my line of country, anyway," the man said. "I'm mostly here doing chauffeur duty for my mother-in-law."

Jessy pulled the tab on her Mountain Dew and made sure the little metal flap was tucked in tidily.

"What are you selling?" asked the bald man.

Jessy didn't see what business it was of his. "Furniture mostly," Matt said. "Our great-uncle left my mother a house, but no money, so we're going to see what the furniture'll fetch."

"I hope she's got a good job," said the bald man. "It's a bad time to inherit real estate, let me tell you!"

"She and Dad'll have to get jobs. We're from Wichita."

"Wichita?" He looked suddenly interested. "This great-uncle of yours, he wasn't old Matthew Holz, was he?"

"Yes, sir," said Matt. "How did you know?"

"Well, son-of-a-gun!" He didn't look much pleased. "I told—did your Aunt Lucy tell your mom about a prospective buyer?"

"I don't think so," said Matt.

"I told her ... Oh, well, I guess she forgot. When Matthew sold me the land for the Green Pastures Apartments, I told him I'd take that last bit anytime he was ready to sell; and when he died I made Miz Holden an offer, knowing she wouldn't care to keep the place up all by herself. She told me he'd left it to his niece in Wichita, but she'd have her call me."

"Mom doesn't want to sell. She wants to live here."

"Well, good luck to her," said the bald man, doubtfully, "but the job market's downright depressed right now."

He cheered up some. "Nope, this is not the city to come to if you want to earn enough to make property taxes and raise a family."

Jessy wished he would go away, but he stayed and told Matt how bad the job market was, how hard older properties were to maintain, and how much less trouble it was to live in an apartment or a condo than a house. When the bald man finally finished his Dr Pepper and left, Matt kicked the grass with his heels and said, "How much of that do you guess is true? About not being able to find a job? And house repairs?"

Jessy shook her head vigorously.

"I bet he just wants to discourage us," said Matt. "You think maybe he knows about the treasure and wants it himself?"

Jessy nodded at the first part and shrugged at the second.

They saw the bald man again after the auction, on their way to the office for their money. He was pushing his mother-in-law in a wheelchair while she talked to another woman; but he excused himself to come over with a big smile on his face, greeting Matt first and then Marly and Daddy. "I don't know if Miz Holden ever got around to mentioning me," he said. "I'm the one bought the property for the Green Pastures Apartments off your Uncle Matthew a while back. I was real sorry to hear he'd passed on."

"Yeah, I bet," said Matt softly in Jessy's ear.

Marly stretched her mouth in a fake smile. "Thank you. I think Great-Aunt Lucy did say something about you."

"Ran into your kids a while back. You've got real nice kids, ma'am. Little girl looks just like you."

Jessy giggled, but nobody corrected him.

"They were saying to me you planned to hang on to the property and try to live there. Is that right?"

"That's exactly right," said Marly.

"Well, good luck. But I wonder if you've considered—"

Jessy leaned against the wall and stopped listening. She didn't like this man, though he hadn't done anything in particular. She hadn't been in the Green Pastures Apartments, but Curtis said they were tiny, and Great-Aunt Lucy said it was hard to get used to hearing other people's TV sets through the walls. Jessy didn't see why he wanted to build any more tiny, thin-walled apartments.

Daddy found an opening in the bald man's talk and said, "Well, I don't think there's any kind of hurry. We'll bear you in mind if it doesn't work out, but you never know what you can do till you try." He took the bald man's business card.

Marly looked after him with her nose wrinkled as he went back to his mother-in-law. "Vampire! Great-Aunt Lucy told me he was at Great-Uncle Matthew's funeral, bugging her to sell. As if there weren't plenty of places to put up his trashy apartments without taking ours!"

"I expect ours would be convenient," said Daddy. "Building trashy apartments is his job, honey; he can't support his mother-in-law's auction habit without it."

"Hmph," said Marly. "Let's go see how much money we made."

Marly looked at the check the clerk gave her, and her

face was very, very still. Daddy looked at it, folded it up in his shirt pocket with the bald man's card, and said nothing. They got all the way to the car in silence; then Matt, as if unable to stay quiet longer, asked, "So how much is it?"

"Not enough," said Marly flatly.

"I knew things were going cheap," said Daddy, buckling himself into the driver's side. "I could tell the day was going slowly, but—" He touched the back of Marly's neck under the layer of heavy brown hair. "It'll be all right. We'll look at the accounts book when we get home and do a little arithmetic."

"It's not enough," said Marly. "It's about half what Rachel thought we ought to get."

"We'll be all right," Daddy repeated stubbornly.

Nobody (except the radio) said a word all the way home. It was past time to start supper, evening was closing in under the trees; but Marly and Daddy went straight to the desk in the living room where Great-Uncle Matthew had kept his accounts book. Matt sat on the back porch with Clyde. Jessy sat on the screen porch with Goldie. Goldie kept chewing on nothing and occasionally opening her mouth to stick her flat gray tongue out. Jessy heard Marly crying in the living room.

After a while, Daddy made steak and noodles. Marly had washed her face, leaving it pink and naked without any makeup. She was smiling, but she didn't fool anybody. "Well, now we know where we stand," she said. "I'd let my hopes get too high, but once you get over the disappointment, it's not that bad, really."

"How bad is it, then?" asked Matt.

"It isn't even really bad," said Marly. "Just not as good as we want it to be. We can't pay the taxes on the property and keep all of us fed and clothed unless Tad and I both get jobs. Soon. Well, we knew we'd have to do that, anyway, right?"

Matt frowned. "I hear the job market's not too good in San Antonio right now," he said, sounding very grown-up.

"It's not, but we can look." Daddy smiled almost as bravely as Marly. "All these cousins in high places you've got, dear, somebody's bound to hire you."

"The worst that can happen," said Marly, "is that neither one of us finds work by the last week in August. That's as late as we can put off telling the school in Wichita that Tad's not coming back. Otherwise, we'll just have to"—she swallowed—"put the property up for sale and move back. We won't be any worse off than before. In fact, we'll be better off. We'll rent a house, and . . . and it'll be all right."

She didn't mean it, though. Marly didn't want to go back to Wichita any more than she wanted to live on the moon, thought Jessy. And what would happen if Marly got a job in San Antonio and Daddy didn't? What would happen if Marly decided her job could support the house, and Matt and Goldie, but not Daddy and Jessy?

After dinner she and Daddy did the dishes. Daddy talked about all the work he had to do, starting first thing tomorrow; he and Marly had to go job hunting, and the house needed to be put back in order now that all the excess furniture was gone, and he'd promised Great-Aunt Lucy to give her some leftover stain and varnish for a project she wanted to do. Jessy nodded a lot, wondering if he were also wondering what would happen if Marly got a job and he didn't.

When they finished the dishes she returned to the screen porch. Matt sat in the recliner talking to Goldie. "Matt," he said. "Matt."

"Bank," said Goldie. "Ghost bank."

"Not bank; Matt," said Matt impatiently. "They don't sound a bit alike, you stupid bird."

"Goldie is a treasure bird," said the parrot.

Jessy, careful to keep her fingers outside the bars, jingled the bells gently. "Hi, squirt," said Matt. "Want me to teach her your name once she gets mine down?"

Jessy nodded, not looking at him.

"I hope that bald guy was wrong about finding jobs," said Matt. "I could be a paperboy, but I don't think it'd help. I think the only thing that'll help is finding that treasure."

Jessy shrugged.

"That'd solve everything. And Curtis has a real good idea. It's a secret, but you won't tell anybody, will you?"

Jessy shook her head and made a scornful face. He knew good and well she wouldn't!

"Okay. He did a science paper last year on limestone caverns. He says they're all over the place around here, but the entrances are closed off so kids won't get lost in them. And so, what he thinks is, whoever stole the money would've put it in a cave and blocked up the entrance. Isn't that what you'd do, if you had a treasure? It's easier than digging a hole; easier to find again, too."

Jessy thought about that. It wasn't a bad idea. In fact, it was a great idea! "B-but why di-didn't Gr-gr—"

"Why didn't Great-Uncle Matthew take it? I don't know." Matt sighed crossly. "I still think there must've been a treasure map or something. I hope we didn't just accidentally sell it. Anyway, we'll have to get busy, if we want to find it before August. You wouldn't believe how many places there are to look for caves on this creek!"

"Creek," said Goldie. "Cross creek. Nobody listens to Goldie."

At least Matt had something useful to do, Jessy thought as she went up to bed. She knelt on her windowsill, feeling the soft evening breeze on her face. It was nice getting undressed with the windows open, not worrying about anybody seeing her. The lighted bulk of the apartments was starting to look awfully ugly to her, though.

Maybe she should look for the treasure. She was beginning to believe in it, just because it was something she could feel hopeful about. After all, if Great-Uncle Matthew didn't know about a treasure, why had he talked about it so much?

On the other hand, why didn't he do anything? Jessy wondered, pulling down the quilt and lying on top of the sheets. Why leave the house to Marly, who didn't have enough money to keep it; and Goldie to Matt, who didn't know anything about parrots; and samplers to her, who wasn't even related? Even if he had left them a treasure map—Jessy sat up. A map! Knocking Jump over in her haste, she turned on the reading lamp and knelt on the pillow to look at the "Home Sweet Home" sampler.

She studied all three samplers inch by inch, but all the threads looked equally old and faded. There were no extra ink or pencil marks on the cloth, no carvings to hide secret panels on the frame, and—when she took it down and turned it over—nothing on the cardboard back. Well, rats! It'd been such a good idea, too. She hung the framed samplers up again. "Seek and ye shall find," said the red letters along the top; but seek where?

"Talk is silver, silence gold," said the left-hand side.

"Talk is gold," said Goldie, inside Jessy's head, and "Ghost bank."

Goldie is a treasure bird.

Nobody listens to Goldie.

What do parrots make you think of? *Treasure Island*, pirates, hidden gold.

Gold hidden in a ghost bank?

Jessy stared at the samplers, thinking furiously, but all she could decide was that she should visit Great-Aunt Lucy tomorrow.

6/
Jigsaw

THE HOUSE seemed even bigger without all the excess furniture. Marly decided she and Daddy should move upstairs, to the front bedroom that had been the master bedroom when the house was first built, and convert the downstairs bedroom back into a parlor. She said that when Great-Uncle Matthew's mother was a teenager the double doors between the two downstairs front rooms would be thrown open for parties, the carpet would be rolled up, and all the neighbors would come to dance. That would be better than the teenager parties that used to happen at the apartments in Wichita, Jessy thought. The music wouldn't bother the neighbors, and you could invite a lot more people than if you had to crowd them just into one room. She wondered if she would have enough friends, by the time she was in high school, to have parties. It might even be worth the effort of making friends, if they could keep this house so she could do it right.

Jessy volunteered to take the stain and varnish over to Great-Aunt Lucy after lunch, when Daddy had gone for a job interview and Marly was resting after calling about jobs and moving furniture all morning. The day was windless, and even the ceiling and window fans in each room did nothing more than move the hot air around. If the weather was like this when the robbers hid the money, then Curtis was probably right about them not wanting to dig a hole. They probably went down into the creek to get cool, and left the gold just so they wouldn't have to carry it.

A path, made mostly of overlapping sneaker and paw-prints, led through the stubby trees that—according to the sampler—were growing where once corn had grown. Jessy had gone this way a couple of times before. Now she paid more attention than usual to the land she walked over, trying to connect something here and now with the "Home Sweet Home" map. The more Jessy thought about it, the surer she was that the sampler had something to do with the treasure; but she couldn't see how something so different from current reality could be useful.

The ford was a shallow place in the creek's deep, narrow bed. The bank on both sides was worn and grassless, with thick gray tree roots poking through the ground to make irregular steps. This was where the cattle had been brought across, Jessy remembered, imagining huge blubbery-nosed animals lumbering up and down the banks, turning the water to mud. There would have been trees here back then, too, maybe even the same trees, since the cottonwoods and hackberry that grew along here now were tall. They trapped the air, cooling it in the shade above the water, which ran clear and silent between the stepping-stones. Well, not quite clear. Somebody'd thrown down a styrofoam cup. Jessy crossed on the broad, nearly flat stones and picked up the cup with a couple of fingers she could spare from holding the stain can. Somewhere, out of sight but not far, Clyde barked. Wouldn't Matt and Curtis be surprised, Jessy thought, if I found the treasure first?

She imagined this pleasantly while crossing the sparse, dry grass to the apartments (*Matt would introduce her to his friends as "the one who found the treasure"*), past a group of girls jumping rope in the parking lot (*Marly would hug her so tight she couldn't breathe and say, "Oh, thank you, Jessy! Now we can all stay here forever!"*), down the narrow sidewalk between the boxy yellow brick buildings, where high-fenced patios were eternally in shade (*Daddy wouldn't say anything, because he wouldn't have to; his face would shine like the sun*), all the way to Great-Aunt Lucy's door.

The door was gray, with a bronze plastic 15A above the peephole. White curtains blocked the aluminum-framed window beside it. The only sounds were the distant chanting of the rope-jumpers and the dull hum of the air-conditioning units, which stuck out nearly to the side-walk, as big and gray as tanks. Before Jessy could find the treasure, she had to understand her clues. Before she could understand her clues, she had to go behind that gray door and ask Great-Aunt Lucy questions. Even in school, Jessy never asked questions. She waited for some-body else to ask; and if nobody else asked, she just never found out.

If Jessy hadn't had the cans of stain and varnish, she might have turned around and gone home; but it was a little, just a little, more embarrassing to take them back than it was to carry on, so she rang the doorbell. She didn't have to ask Great-Aunt Lucy anything, anyway. She probably wouldn't be any help.

Great-Aunt Lucy opened the door with her wrinkles all turning down, but as soon as she saw Jessy they turned upward. "Why, hi there, Jessy! You brung me that stuff your Daddy promised? That's right nice of you. You come on in."

Jessy stepped into the entryway and was immediately cold. The air-conditioning was up way too high. A little square of hall between the door and the closet was covered in plastic tiles; then after a rim of aluminum, the sort-of gray, sort-of brown carpet began. One side opened onto a little bedroom about the size of Jessy's room in Wichita, and the other side opened onto a living room and kitchen a lot like the Wichita living room and kitchen. Jessy wasn't sure why she suddenly felt like she'd walked into a shrinking box; it should have seemed familiar and ordinary. Great-Aunt Lucy took her into the living room, where the cold air smelled like cleanser and carrot cake, and let in a little warmth as she opened the sliding glass doors to put the cans out on her patio. The furniture was made of light wood with smooth, pink-flowered upholstery, and looked too big for the space. As Jessy took the Styrofoam cup into the kitchen to throw away, she saw a jigsaw puzzle spread out on the breakfast bar; one of the really hard ones, with trees and a mountain reflected in a lake.

"I'm real sorry to hear you didn't get as much money for that furniture as you needed," said Great-Aunt Lucy, closing the patio doors. "It's a crying shame how little good furniture'll fetch; and you can bet it was all bought up by dealers who'll charge other folks three times what they paid for it. But life is hard and there's no saying different. Would you like some milk and carrot cake? I just made it this morning. I never used to feel like baking in the summer, but I get so chilly here sometimes with that air-conditioning up so high—the thermostat's no good, it's all controlled by some silly computer—I get a real hankering for a hot stove. There's no way I can eat it all myself, so any time you or Matt get a mind to you can come over and help me out."

Jessy nodded and made room for Great-Aunt Lucy in the kitchen. It was only a kitchenette, really, about half the size of the one in Wichita, so that must be what was making her feel closed in. She sat on a bar stool and looked at the puzzle. All the edge pieces had been put together like a frame, and some parts of the inside picture had been assembled and were sitting around at random.

"Do you like jigsaw puzzles?" asked Great-Aunt Lucy. "Matthew and I used to do them for hours; only he was faster at them than me. He could see the way pieces fit that didn't look like they had anything to do with the same part of the picture."

Jessy accepted a plate of carrot cake with a big dab of whipped topping and a glass of milk. She wondered how to find out what she needed to know without just blurting out questions, which seemed crude and embarrassing.

Great-Aunt Lucy blinked a couple of times as she sat on the other bar stool. "Poor Matthew. It's a shame you didn't know him better. Most of the youngest nieces and nephews annoyed him. Said they didn't have any brains or gumption or common sense. He took a shine to you and Matt, though. I think it was the way you were so nice and quiet around Goldie, and Matt stood up for you to the other kids. He liked your daddy, too. After the reunion he said to me, 'Looks like Marly did okay by herself the second time around.' " She ate carrot cake and tried a piece of mountain against the sky, and then against the water.

Jessy swallowed, and spoke as slowly as she could, pretending to try to find a place for a tree piece. "G-goldie t-talks for me real well," she said. "M-matt's trying to t-teach her his name, b-but all sh-she says is 'b-bank.' "

Great-Aunt Lucy laughed. "Isn't that just like her! Matthew loved that old bird something awful, but she could be a trial. I thought he was out of his mind when he bought her, she cost so much, but I guess it was worth it to him."

"Wh-when did he g-get her?" Jessy laid down the tree piece and picked up one with a ripple of water.

"Oh, let's see. My husband was still alive, and Matthew hadn't sold off much land yet. I used to run out to see him every week or so. One day I come in and there's this big old bird in the middle of the living room. Seems one of our old hands from Mexico went into the parrot business, and he'd dropped by on his way through town one day. That's where all these green-and-yellow type parrots come from—Mexico. And he had this parrot with him. Matthew said they took a liking to each other right off, and he got her real reasonable." Great-Aunt Lucy made a sound between a sniff and a laugh. "It wasn't his usual idea of reasonable, though, let me tell you! I don't know how many hundreds of dollars he wound up spending, plus her food and vet bills and cage and all."

"D-did he t-teach her t-to t-talk all himself?" asked

Jessy, realizing that what she'd thought was a ripple of water was really a shadow on the mountain, and putting it in place.

"Every word. I think she could say *ola* when he got her. That's Spanish for hello. He said he was going to teach her to recite poetry, but it's hard for her to get long sentences into the right order. He had to teach her everything in little bits, and say everything over and over and over, real slow." Great-Aunt Lucy pushed a mat of puzzle pieces against the frame, where it snapped into place. "And you know, his stutter went away, even though he'd had it forever! I said to him, 'Matthew, if I'd known it'd do that, I'd've gotten you a parrot my ownself, years ago!'"

Jessy put two tree pieces together. "Wh-what all did he t-teach her to s-say?"

"Oh, all sorts of things. A lot of it didn't make any sense to me."

"Gh-ghost b-bank?"

"Yes, that sort of thing. What on earth is a ghost bank? Or a—what was it she'd say?—a gay tank? Some of it's her garbling words. If she gets excited she can't talk straight. Plus, some letters are hard for her, like *f* and *p* and *m*."

"Wh-what k-kind of little b-bits did he t-teach her?" asked Jessy; then she realized from Great-Aunt Lucy's blank look that the question wasn't quite clear. "How l-long was each s-sentence?"

"Oh, real short," said Great-Aunt Lucy. "Not even a whole sentence, usually. You have to divide it into syllables instead of words, and you teach her two or three, and then get her to combine them. Like he taught her 'treasure bird' and 'Goldie is a' separately, and then he taught her to put them together."

"Wh-why did he t-teach her that?" asked Jessy.

Great-Aunt Lucy shrugged. "Who knows? I think because parrots made him think of pirates and pirates made him think of treasure. Matthew always had a funny way of thinking that nobody else could follow. Like, when he'd hide Easter eggs, he'd think he was putting them out in plain sight. He'd put them in the icebox, or in with the other eggs in the chicken house, or tie a yellow egg to the yellow rosebush—now who's going to look there? I swear I must've looked straight at that one six times, and it might be there yet if he hadn't been rolling around on the porch laughing at me about it."

"S-so he was real sm-smart?" Suddenly Jessy found that several groups of three or four pieces she had would go with one Great-Aunt Lucy was doing, to make one big part of the picture.

"I don't know that he was any smarter than the rest of us. He just had a different sort of mind. Devious—and the funny thing is, the simpler he tried to be, the more devious he got!"

"Wh-what's de-de-de-de-vi-ous?" Jessy had to hold her hands still and concentrate on each syllable in order to pronounce the new word.

"It's . . . sneaky. I don't mean mean or dishonest. Matthew was so honest I didn't dare ask him how he liked a new dress! But he thought of things sideways instead of head on." She thought a minute, eating carrot cake. "He never ever broke his word or told a secret. But ask him for directions, and he'd have you all over creation!" Her eyes fixed on the pieces Jessy had assembled. "You know,

I think if we put this piece here, and your bunch of pieces—there!" Suddenly the jigsaw puzzle seemed to shake itself, and Jessy saw that she had been looking at it wrong. She turned the large piece carefully and slid it into place upside-down from where she'd thought it went, so that the puzzle was half done.

"My!" said Great-Aunt Lucy, licking whipped topping off her fork. "That's the last place I expected that to belong! I think these jigsaw puzzle people must have brains like Matthew's." She picked up Jessy's empty plate and cup, and took them to the sink. "I wish you could've known him better. He was kind of a tease, but he was always there when any of us younger ones needed him. And he kept the old place together, which was more than any of the rest of us could do. He was a lot like our daddy. I can't count the number of times when we thought we were going to lose the old place, or go hungry, or not have any Christmas, but Daddy always got the money somewhere. And Matthew did, too."

"So Gr-great-Uncle Matthew w-wouldn't've not th-thought of t-taxes," said Jessy.

"I'm sure he thought of everything he could." Great-Aunt Lucy put the dirty dishes in the dishwasher. "But don't you get your hopes up about golden treasures. Matthew never asked more of life than that he should get by, and he wouldn't've provided any more than that, I wouldn't think. He may have expected the furniture to fetch more than it did, or maybe he didn't have the same ideas of getting by that young folks have now."

Jessy couldn't think of anything to say to that, and she couldn't think of any more to ask, and she had goose bumps on her bare legs. She got down from the bar stool.

"Th-thank you f-for the c-cake," she said. "I b-better go home now."

"You're welcome anytime," said Great-Aunt Lucy brightly. "Let me wrap up some carrot cake for Matt, and your mom and dad."

"She's n-not my mom," said Jessy.

Some of Great-Aunt Lucy's wrinkles turned down. "I know that, honey, but she's like your mother now."

Jessy shook her head. "She said I d-didn't have to c-call her that. M-mommy and M-marly aren't the same at all!"

"Oh. Well. I didn't mean—" Great-Aunt Lucy fluttered as she wrapped up the cake. "Do you see your mother often?"

"Pr-probably never, anym-more." Jessy stared at Great-Aunt Lucy, daring her to feel sorry for her.

"Oh, how sad!" Great-Aunt Lucy gave her the soft, plastic-wrapped bundle. "I'm sorry to hear that."

Jessy took the bundle and stuck out her chin. "I l-like M-marly better, anyway."

She hadn't meant to say that; and poor Great-Aunt Lucy looked so horrified she wished she hadn't. Jessy had had enough of talking for one day. She let herself out the door into the hot, bright afternoon, and went home to start a clue notebook.

7/Clues

JESSY SAT cross-legged in the recliner, with a legal pad in her lap, and chewed on the end of her pencil. Goldie chewed, too, contentedly peeling bark off a twig. Jessy wished that Goldie understood English, instead of just being able to repeat it. She was absolutely certain that Great-Uncle Matthew had taught Goldie to give directions for finding the treasure; but as far as the bird was concerned, all the treasure-finding phrases were as meaningless as "Gig 'em Aggies." So Jessy was writing down all the phrases she could remember hearing Goldie say, hoping some of them would turn into sense when put together and looked at the right way, like jigsaw puzzle pieces.

Some words, like *Matthew* and *hello*, were obvious, the sort of thing any parrot would learn to say; that was column one. Others, like *Goldie is a treasure bird* and *Talk is gold*, seemed to point in the right direction; that was column two. Column three, phrases that made no sense and so might well be real clues, was depressingly short. *Ghost bank* was the only thing she could think of for a long time; then she put down *gay tank* because Great-Aunt Lucy had remembered it. Finally, she recalled that Goldie sometimes said, "Cross creek" when Matt said "creek," so she put that down.

She drew a picture of a girl's face at the top of the page, trying to think deviously. Creeks had banks. Banks were where people stored their money. But why "ghost bank?" And if you had to cross the creek to get the gold, you might as well not bother. Great-Uncle Matthew had sold all the land across the creek to the bald-headed man, and anything found there would belong to him.

The ponytails Jessy was putting on the girl's head spread out and turned into a wreath. Of course, you could take the gold out of a cave on the apartment side of the creek, put it into a cave on the house side, but that would be stealing. If Great-Uncle Matthew were as honest as Great-Aunt Lucy said he was—and she ought to know—he wouldn't give them directions to steal.

The wreath spread out and turned into a box. Maybe the money would belong to Marly, whoever found it. It would have belonged to Great-Uncle Matthew's mother when Lamar died, if anybody had known where to find it, and then to Great-Uncle Matthew, and then—no, he'd left all the money to Great-Aunt Lucy. That could still solve the problem, if Great-Aunt Lucy could maybe buy the house from Marly and rent it to them; but it seemed kind of complicated. Maybe it wouldn't to a devious mind, though. She wrote a note on the bottom of the page: "Who owns the money if it's found where?"

She heard Matt, Curtis, and Clyde coming, and stuck the pad down beside the recliner cushion. They had their ideas, and she had hers. When she found the treasure first, Matt would see she wasn't some dumb kid he had to be nice to. She heard the back door slam, and Matt yell, "Hey, Jess! What you want for lunch?"

Jessy jingled Goldie's bells good-bye, went to the kitchen, and pointed haughtily to the SpaghettiOs on the counter.

"Heck, she could've fixed that herself," said Curtis, sprawling against the table with his elbows on a large, grubby piece of manila paper.

"Mom said for me to fix her lunch, so I'm fixing it," said Matt. "I shouldn't even've left her by herself all morning."

"If my sister was this helpless, I'd shoot her," said Curtis.

Jessy stuck her nose in the air and got down the shallow, old-fashioned soup bowls; not the Depression-glass ones, which had been sold, but the ones with the weird blue flowers on the bottom. She wondered why nobody made these kinds of soup bowls anymore. They were perfect to eat SpaghettiOs out of, because you didn't lose all the sauce, like you did on a plate.

"It's too bad that one cave was on the wrong side of the creek," said Matt, opening the can. "It would've made a great robber's den."

"Yeah. We could fix it up, you know? Camp there."

"I don't have time to go camping," said Matt, dumping the SpaghettiOs into a saucepan. "You've got the rest of your life to look for this treasure, but if I don't find it by mid-August, I'm sunk."

"Some sunk," said Curtis, moving the manila paper so

Jessy could set his place. "Your mom said you'd get to keep the parrot and use the money from selling this place to get a house, right?"

"If we can sell it," said Matt. "She doesn't want to sell to developers, and who else is going to buy?"

"Yeah, but one way or another you'll move back to some nice neighborhood." Curtis went to the refrigerator for a Coke. "If my mom gets laid off, we may have to move back in with my grandmother, and next thing you know I'll be in a gang."

"Oh, bull," said Matt, turning the stove up and stirring the SpaghettiOs. "If you are it'll be your own fault."

"No it won't. The gangs at that school, they make you belong. Otherwise, you get your face bashed in."

Jessy looked at the manila paper as they talked. Matt or Curtis—probably Curtis, since the lines were so neat—had mapped the creek, marking the caves, deep places, hollow trees, and heavy growth between the highway and the fence that separated the property from their next neighbors, who kept chickens and lived in a trailer till they could build their dream home. Some places were marked with black *x*'s, some with red, and some had little notes: Frog pond, Duck nest, Impassable bamboo. Something didn't look right. Jessy studied the paper, frowning.

"You be careful with that map," said Curtis, as Matt brought the saucepan to the table. "It took me a long time to make that."

Jessy, who had figured out the problem, smiled smugly.

"What's she grinning about?" Curtis asked Matt.

"Who knows?" Small flecks of tomato sauce splattered around the bowls as he poured lunch. "You know, Jess, someday your tongue's going to wither up and fall out from lack of use."

"Don't bug her about it," said Curtis. "I wish my little sister could keep so quiet. Where you want to look after lunch?"

"I don't know. It seems like we already checked out all the good places. I've got this feeling about that bamboo, though."

"Well, you better hope you're wrong, because there's no way we can get through that stuff."

"Wouldn't it be awful if the treasure were under the highway? That's all federal land, you know. The government'd get all that, and the taxes too."

Curtis shook his head. "It's not under the highway. They'd've found it. If you're laying a road, you've got to dig up everything and lay a roadbed. Jessy, stop shaking the table."

Jessy was sure the way she was swinging her feet could not possibly be jiggling the table, and Matt and Curtis needed taking down some. "Th-that map's no g-good," she said, swinging harder.

"Shows what you know," said Matt. "We copied it off the map of the apartments in the office, and then walked from one end of the creek to the other, making corrections."

"It's st-still wr-wrong." Jessy smirked.

"Oh, don't pay any attention to her," said Curtis. "She's probably being a pain because we're not inviting her."

Jessy put on the best superior face she could manage, and Matt looked doubtful. "She usually never talks unless she's got a better reason than that," he said.

Jessy nodded.

"Well, if she's got a reason she'd better spit it out," said Curtis. "We don't have time to play stupid little-girl games."

"You're right." Matt nodded. "We've got important stuff to do, Jess, so unless you want to go back to Wichita this fall, you can just leave us alone."

Jessy didn't see any reason to sit still for that. She snatched up the map and ran, sprinting upstairs with the boys shouting behind her. She hurled herself into her room, bounced feet first onto the unmade bed, and held the map next to her samplers. The difference was obvious: One section of the creek was missing a great big curve on the boys' map.

"Come on, squirt, stop playing stupid games," said Matt.

She jabbed the paper map with her finger, then the sampler, then the paper again. Matt came closer, Curtis hovering in the doorway. "Give it on back and stop being a brat."

Jessy sighed heavily. "Are you bl-blind?" she asked.

Matt rolled his eyes. "Yes, I can see you've got a map, too, but—hey, Curtis! Take a look at this!"

Curtis came all the way into the room. "It's a bunch of embroidery. So what?"

"It's a map," said Matt slowly. "A map of this property. Great-Uncle Matthew left it to Jessy. Remember how I thought there must be a treasure map somewhere?"

Curtis examined the map more closely. "That's not a treasure map. It's too old." He pointed to the date in the corner.

"Yeah, but look at this part of the creek." Matt pointed.

"This shows a deep curve where our map shows it straight. It's hard to tell right where it's supposed to be, but there isn't any bend like that anywhere."

Curtis studied both maps. "Son-of-a-gun," he said. "I bet sometime or other since that was made a flood came along or something, and the creekbed changed. That happens, you know. I read about it when I was doing my geology paper. Jess, you may be a brat, but you got good eyes. It may not mean anything, though."

Matt's eyes were all lit up. "I bet it does," he said. "It's got to be a clue. That's why he went to all the trouble to make sure somebody got the sampler instead of just selling it off. And look what it says up top—'Seek and ye shall find.' And this other one's got money on it. It's got to be a clue!"

"Well, what are we waiting for then?" demanded Curtis.

"I'm g-going, t-too!" said Jessy, hopping off the bed and making the floor shake with the force of her landing.

Forgetting lunch, they raced downstairs, snatching the boys' treasure-hunting kit—a backpack full of emergency survival equipment like tape measures, flashlights, and Great-Aunt Lucy's oatmeal raisin cookies—off the back porch on the way out. Clyde, who had been all ready to stretch out for a rest in the shade, forced himself to his feet again and came, too, catching the excitement as they pelted down the path to the ford. There they slid into the creekbed and made their way along the grassy, rocky verge, which now was wide enough for them to go single file, the summer water level being low. Clyde, not caring about wet feet, bounced through the water and barked at turtles.

There was some disagreement about how far they should go. Jessy barely got to express her opinion because neither Matt nor Curtis was patient enough to let her get a whole sentence out, but she was too excited to mind. If a spot had once been part of the creek, and wasn't now, couldn't you call that a "ghost bank?" And maybe, when she saw the place, "cross creek" might make sense, too. If they found the treasure now, she'd never be mad at Matt again! Finding it herself would've been better, but she'd never have thought of making a map of the creek, so she didn't mind if the boys got some of the credit, too.

Matt and Curtis stopped to look at their map and argue about whether a gully cutting into the creek on the family's side, spilling loose stones down the bank, could have been an old creek channel, but Jessy didn't see the point of talking about it. She climbed up to it, mostly on her hands and knees, slipping on the stones and sending them pouring down, along with a sifting of dirt. "Watch it, squirt!" warned Matt, but she pulled herself up by a bare live oak root and stood in the gully with just her head above ground-level on one side, and an outcrop of layered limestone, like a miniature cliff, poking up on the other.

Her heart seemed to have crawled up out of her chest to fill her throat. This had to be right! You couldn't find a better ghost bank than the pale limestone, and it was even on the far side of the gully from the house, so it would have been across the creek if the gully used to be a creekbed. She walked slowly, rocks and stickers hurting her bare feet, and heard Clyde scramble up behind her.

"Come on," Matt said to Curtis. "It won't hurt to look."

The top of the limestone wall was ragged with grass

and Queen Anne's lace growing as tall as Jessy in a thin layer of soil. The rock face was jagged, poking way out into the gully every few feet in all directions—up, down, side-to-side, and then falling back. Clyde pressed his cold nose into the back of Jessy's knee and she stopped to pat him, peering into an overhang where water had washed out a layer of softer earth or stone from under the cliff. The hole didn't go back near deep enough to be a cave.

Curtis and Matt, equipped with sneakers, caught up to and passed Jessy, climbing up and down the gully's sides as they went. "See, if it's a creekbed there should be more trees along here," said Curtis. "Trees always crowd onto creekbeds."

"Not on this side," said Matt from the top of the shelf. "This side there's no dirt to grow in. And on that lower side I bet the trees got cut down or something. Remember, it's been years." He skidded on a rock-strewn slope, and braked to a stop, still well above Jessy's head. "Hey, look here!"

Curtis clambered up and crowded next to him. Their bodies blocked whatever they looked at. "Yeah, that's great! I bet it'd be above the water level and everything."

Clyde barked impatiently, and Jessy agreed with him. She took hold of the uneven rock face to try to pull herself up, but she was too short to grip the right place, and her bare feet were no help. Matt got Curtis's flashlight out of the treasure-finding kit, and crouched, holding it to shine on whatever he was looking at, cupping his free hand around his eyes.

"See anything?" asked Curtis breathlessly as Jessy fell back, frustrated.

"Something . . . something's glittering! It's pretty deep,

too." Matt sat back, shaking his head. "I can't tell. It's too far back. Here, you try."

"H-hey!" yelled Jessy, as he passed Curtis the flashlight. "Wh-what ab-bout m-me!"

Matt looked down. "Sorry, squirt. You want a hand?"

Jessy glared at him for his stupidity, but he reached for her, and she let him haul her up. Curtis was shaking his head over a dark hole in the limestone. "Here, I'll hold the light, and you reach in."

A cave! They'd found a real cave near the top of the shelf—only a small one, but plenty big enough to hide a treasure in. Jessy sat on the edge of the gully with her feet dangling over Clyde's upturned face, holding her breath. Matt reached in, his right arm, his head, his left arm, his shoulders—

"Rats!" He pulled out. "It goes back too far. But there's something in there, all right! I could see a big lump right in the back, before my shoulders stuck. You try."

Curtis was a little skinnier than Matt, but he only got as far in as his shoulder blades. "Dadgum it!" he said. "No wonder Mr. Holz never went after it! It's too little for anybody to get in."

Jessy looked at the black hole in the white stone under the fringe of Queen Anne's lace and measured it with her eyes. It was awfully small. And dark. But, if the gold was in there—she swallowed. "It's n-not t-too sm-small f-for me," she said.

The boys turned and stared at her.

8/Cave

JESSY STARED back, trying not to think about how small and dark the cave was, and all the nasty crawly things she might find in it. She wasn't going to lose the treasure now just because crawling into holes was a little spooky. Or a lot spooky. "You really think you'd fit?" asked Matt.

Jessy shrugged and balanced her way over to them, gripping the steep limestone with bare toes as well as fingers. The boys made way. "She might," said Curtis. "Let her try."

"Okay, but watch it," said Matt, backing off from the hole.

Jessy took hold of the stone rim and put her face down next to the darkness. A smell came out at her, an old, dry smell unlike anything she was familiar with. The hole looked even darker up close. She poked her hands in first, then her arms, feeling the floor, which sloped downward from the lowest part of the entrance and was covered with something dry and rustly. The ceiling was low, but not too low to crawl under if she was careful, and she couldn't feel walls on either side. She swallowed, and thrust in her head and shoulders.

The fabric of her tank top dragged on the rocks above and below as she wiggled forward, her feet flailing loosely in the air till one of the boys caught them and gave her something to push against. Head low, unable to see, she pulled her hips forward—almost stuck—popped through and was in, the floor rustling like leaves beneath her. All she could see was darkness ahead and the light from the entrance immediately around her. "P-p-pass me the fl-flashlight," she called, sounding small and scared to herself; but that was silly. Nothing here was going to hurt her, and she was about to be a hero.

She couldn't actually see who blocked the light, but it was Matt's voice that said, "Here. Can you reach it?"

Jessy wiggled in a circle, groping toward the sound, and bumped her head on the ceiling before she found the warm metal tube wrapped within a sweaty hand. She got a good grip and tugged, feeling for the switch as Matt let go. When it snapped on, the light shone full on Matt's face, which scrunched up against the brightness and withdrew suddenly with a loud, "Ow! Watch it, squirt!"

"That thing in the back," called Curtis. "What is it?"

The beam of light wobbled over the walls and ceiling as she rolled, trying to get into a good position. Whatever was on the floor was kind of scratchy, but it was the ceiling that worried her. She didn't have room even to get on her hands and knees and crawl properly, though there was plenty of space to turn around in if she lay flat. She wriggled her elbows underneath her, raising her head slightly and trying to position the flashlight so she could see the back of the cave, still several feet away.

"Well?" Curtis sounded impatient. "What is it?"

"G-give me a m-minute," said Jessy crossly. Something had sparkled back there! "You m-mean th-that big wh-white l-lump?"

"That's it! Is it the jar of gold?"

It took Jessy a minute to crawl forward and touch the object, to be sure of her identification. Her eyes were addled from the combination of darkness and light. It was about the right shape for a jar—but no. She felt the disappointment all through her, and shook her head.

"Jessy! Talk, for crying out loud!" Matt sounded as breathless as Curtis.

"It's j-just a rock," said Jessy. "W-with shiny fl-flakes."

"Shiny flakes?" Matt's voice was quieter talking to Curtis. "Could it be some kind of ore sample?"

"No way," said Curtis firmly. "Lots of rocks have little glittery pieces. You wouldn't get ore in this limestone around here. I looked it up for my science paper."

I hope he got an A plus on that paper, thought Jessy. He put everything in it but the kitchen sink. She moved the light to cover the back wall. Nothing but rock, poking out in layers. She swung the beam for a look at the sides.

"Shine the light on around, Jess," called Matt. "Maybe there's something off to the side."

"And the floor," added Curtis.

"I wish you'd talk," said Matt. "It's not fair, you knowing what's going on and us not."

She hadn't thought of the floor. What if the gold were scattered like gravel? Eagerly, she swept aside the rustly stuff and swung the light lower—onto a complicated pile of snakes.

Jessy's breath choked her. Snakes! They were everywhere—all over the floor—dry and rustly—she dropped the flashlight and banged her head on the roof as she tried to back up the slope, feeling the crunch of snakeskin under her knees, under her hands. "Sn-sn-sn-sn—" She tried to yell, but her mouth betrayed her as usual. She pivoted on her stomach and scrambled toward daylight, still trying to yell, scream, do something to let the boys know what trouble she was in! "He-he-he—"

Her head and arms emerged into daylight and Matt reached for her. "Jess, what's the matter?"

"Sn-sn-sn-sn—" Her hips stuck! She kicked frantically, stubbing her toes on rocks, feeling the dry scaly snakes scattering down the slope as she tried to push free.

"What's the matter?" demanded Curtis, as Matt took one arm.

"It's no use asking, with her like this. Help me pull!"

After a while, Jessy got a grip on her jaws and was able to answer Matt's and Curtis's questions. "Sn-sn-snakes," she gasped. "H-h-h-undreds of sn-sn-snakes, and n-no g-gold!"

"Snakes?" said Curtis blankly. "A snake wouldn't be inside his den this time of year."

"I s-s-s-saw them," said Jessy.

"Them? You sure?"

Jessy nodded.

"You sure it wasn't just a bunch of cast-off skins?" asked Matt.

"I didn't hear rattling," said Curtis. "What color were they?"

Jessy shrugged. She was starting to feel silly. Most snakes weren't dangerous. She'd learned that in school, and seen it on TV, and read it in her nature books; so why had it scared her so badly to be in the cave with them? But there had seemed to be so many of them—

"Grass snakes, I bet," said Curtis in disgust. "I bet it was a bunch of grass snakes. Or maybe it was an old den and there weren't any snakes, just skins." He looked around. "Hey, what'd you do with that flashlight? Did you drop it in there?"

Jessy looked at her hands. She couldn't remember dropping the flashlight, but she didn't have it now. Curtis muttered something and climbed back up to poke his head into the hole. "Don't see it," he said, pulling out. "If you lost it—"

Suddenly Jessy wanted to cry; but she wasn't going to. She'd die first. Blinking, she smoothed the front of her tank top, and winced at the touch. Her shorts were filthy, and her tank top was torn, and her stomach and legs were scraped from the rocks.

"Lay off, Curt," said Matt. "She didn't mean to drop it. She just got scared."

"Of a bunch of old snakeskins," grumbled Curtis. "I got a handful—they're a bunch of bull snake skins. That was my old man's flashlight. He'll kill me."

"I'll help you look for it, okay?" Matt helped Jessy to her feet, as if she couldn't do it by herself. "We better get you cleaned up before Mom or Tad-the-Dad sees you."

"Wh-what ab-bout the tr-tr—"

"We can finish exploring later," said Matt. "Come on. We never even had lunch. No wonder we screwed up. We didn't have a plan or anything."

They returned more slowly than they had come, Matt and Curtis talking over Jessy's head. At home Jessy washed her scrapes and painted herself with disinfectant while Matt reheated the cold SpaghettiOs and Curtis tramped upstairs, where she soon found he had carefully copied the missing creek bend from the sampler to his own map, putting it in with dotted lines and question marks.

"It's a bummer the gold wasn't there," he said, as he shoveled in his spaghetti. "I thought we had something."

"We may still," said Matt. "We'll go back right after lunch."

Jessy nodded vigorously, feeling better with something in her stomach. Just because the treasure wasn't in the first cave they'd seen didn't mean she hadn't figured the clues right.

"Not you, squirt," said Matt. "You've been enough trouble for one day."

Trouble! "Y-you n-never w-would've found the gu-gully without m-me!"

"You're too little for treasure hunting," said Curtis.

"T-ten's not li-little!"

Curtis looked at Matt in surprise. "She's ten?"

"Hard to believe, isn't it?" said Matt. "I think she stopped growing when she stopped talking."

Jessy glared. "You c-can't st-stop me, you know."

"Actually that's true," Curtis said to Matt. "Unless we can lock her in her room."

Jessy gave them a look that dared them to, and Matt backed down from it. "We better not," he said. "She might tie sheets together and climb out the window and break her neck, and then I'd get the blame." He turned to Jessy. "But you get shoes on, and change your clothes. Mom'll have a fit when she sees the ones you're wearing."

"Wear jeans," instructed Curtis. "They'll protect your legs from more scrapes. You really tore yourself up there."

So Jessy suffered, sweating, in jeans and sneakers and her oldest T-shirt all afternoon. They traced the course of the gully back into the fields as well as they could, but the limestone shelf ran out before they found any more suitable treasure holes. They couldn't even find Curtis's flashlight, so when it came time to quit, he went home muttering about little kids who couldn't take care of things.

The car was in the drive as they returned, and Daddy was coming out on the back porch to call them. "Where've you been?" he asked.

"Treasure hunting," said Matt. "How'd the job hunting go?"

Daddy shrugged. "I expect my day was about as effective as yours. Marly's got a strong lead, though. Who drank up all the lemonade and didn't make more?"

They didn't have a chance to answer, because as they entered the kitchen, Marly did, too, flourishing Jessy's tank top. "Tad, look at—there you are! Mind telling me what happened to this?"

"Oh, cripes, Jessy, can't you put your clothes in the hamper like everybody else?" moaned Matt.

Jessy shrugged. She'd been in a hurry, and how was she to know Marly would come barging into her room looking for her?

"It looks like she's been mauled by a tiger," said Daddy.

"It caught on some rocks while she was exploring a possible treasure cave," said Matt. "It's no big deal."

"What was she doing? Using her stomach for a tobog-gan?" Marly raised her hand. "No, Matt, let Jessy tell me about it."

Jessy took a deep breath and spoke very slowly. Why was Marly so big on making her talk? "I expl-plored a c-cave and got st-stuck on the w-way out."

"Got stuck? How big a cave?" asked Daddy.

"I w-was the only one who'd f-fit."

"She volunteered," said Matt. "We thought we saw the treasure jar, and we had to be sure. It was her own fault she got stuck. She didn't have any trouble getting in, but on the way out she panicked and got herself all scraped up."

"Scraped up?" said Daddy. "Honey, are you hurt?"

"Panicked?" said Marly. "Why should she panic?"

So then they had to explain about the snakeskins, and Jessy had to pull up her shirt and show the damage to her stomach, and Matt even let slip about the loss of Curtis's dad's flashlight; which just went to show, in Jessy's opinion, that talking wasn't all it was cracked up to be. The more used you were to talking, the more likely you were to say something better left unsaid. Matt, for some reason, was in worse trouble than she was; he got a long lecture on responsibility, and near as nothing got grounded from treasure hunting. Jessy didn't think that was fair.

"He c-couldn't st-stop me," she pointed out. "And wh-what if it had b-been the tr-treasure? You'd be gl-glad as anyb-body."

So they got a long list of new rules about treasure hunting, and that was the end of it, except that nobody was in a good mood that evening, and after Jessy got ready for bed and Daddy and Marly saw the state of her legs—which the jeans had rubbed raw—they almost got mad all over again. Matt, however, had shut himself in his room with a lot of treasure-hunting magazines he'd borrowed from Curtis, and it wasn't worth the effort of hauling him out for another scolding.

When Matt, who went to bed half an hour later than Jessy, came past her open door on the way to the bathroom, she was lying awake feeling bad and small. She didn't mind much getting scraped up, but it *was* her fault about that and about the flashlight, so she didn't see why everybody was so down on Matt. She wasn't sure what she could do about it now, but she got up and knocked on the bathroom door. "What?" asked Matt, sounding as if he had a mouthful of toothpaste.

Jessy wished he'd open the door; but she couldn't say this with signs anyway. "I'm sorry I g-got you in tr-trouble."

She heard water running, heard him spit. "You didn't. Go back to bed."

"I d-did, t-too."

"Okay, fine. You did. So what? I can take it better than you can. Go to bed before Mom or Tad-the-Dad catch you."

Jessy couldn't think of anything to say to that, so she went back to bed, and lay on top of the covers with the fan blowing on her, staring out the window at the lighted bulk of the apartments. After a while she fell asleep, and dreamed she was back in Wichita, only the apartment was smaller and darker than she remembered, just her bedroom and the living room; and she lived there all alone.

9/ Cross

JESSY WAS waiting for Matt when he came to the side porch for his hour with Goldie the next morning. Goldie, her feathers growing back and her eyes bright, was chowing down on a chunk of peach with obvious enjoyment. "Hello," she said. "Treasure bird. Talk is Goldie. Goody-goody."

"Hello, Goldie," said Matt. "You going to say my name today?"

Jessy slid forward in the recliner and held out the legal pad with all her notes on it, poking him with it.

"What is it, Jess?" Matt sighed.

"A l-list of wh-what G-Goldie says," said Jessy. She had awakened that morning with her mind made up. The important thing was finding the treasure in time, not who found it.

Matt took the pad. "Yeah. So? What's with the columns?"

Jessy let him look them over, thinking how to explain her ideas in as few words as possible. "N-notice anything f-funny?"

"Great-Uncle Matthew sure taught her to talk about

the treasure a lot," said Matt. "This last column makes no sense."

"Cl-clues," said Jessy. He looked at her blankly. "Gr-great-Uncle M-matthew t-taught her to say cl-clues!"

"Matthew," said Goldie. "Pretty Matthew. Nobody listens to Goldie!"

Matt turned to gaze at the parrot as she finished her peach and stretched out her wing, impossibly long, for preening. "And then left her to me so I'd figure them out and find it? But that's—I don't know, Jessy. That's pretty complicated."

"D-devious. And th-there's m-my samplers. I b-bet he th-thought he w-was being ob-obvious."

"Your samplers?" Matt did not see them everyday, so he had to think about that. "The 'Home Sweet Home' map—yeah, that looks like a clue; except that creek bit was a bust. What else? 'Seek and ye shall find.' I guess that is plain, when you think about it. What's the other one?"

"T-talk is s-silver, si-lence g-gold."

"Talk is gold," Goldie contradicted.

Matt bent his head closer to the bars. "Yeah, talk is gold. What else? Come on, Goldie, talk is gold. Talk is gold."

"Talk is gold," repeated Goldie. "Never sold. Never sold. Talk is gold."

Jessy clapped her hands. A new phrase!

"You know, you may be on to something," said Matt. "You think that's him telling us for sure the land with the treasure on it was never sold?" He looked at the list. "But then—what does 'cross creek' mean? Everything across the creek was sold."

Jessy shrugged. "Th-the g-gully would've worked gr-great. It's ev-ven a gh-ghost bank."

"Hey, that's right." He looked worried. "I hope that wasn't the right place yesterday, and somebody came along and stole it already! That'd be awful."

It was so awful Jessy didn't want to think about it. "Wh-what's a g-gay t-tank? I n-never h-heard th-that one. Gr-great-Aunt Lucy re-rem—said it."

"I don't know. Maybe she remembered it wrong?" Matt turned to Goldie again. "Okay, girl, how about gay tank? Gay tank?"

"Gay tank," said Goldie, abandoning her grooming and stepping onto the bars. "Gayt ank."

No matter how often they got her to repeat it, they couldn't make sense of it, so they concentrated on the only phrase that seemed to offer any solid directions— "cross creek." "You know, she doesn't say 'across creek,'" said Matt. "Maybe she's not using cross as a verb. It could mean other things, you know."

"Cr-cranky cr-creek." Jessy giggled.

Matt smiled patiently. "Or cross like a church cross, or an *x*. You know, *x* marks the spot?"

Jessy sat bolt upright. "Cr-cr-cr-" Drat her mouth!

Daddy poked his head in while she was still trying to get the word out. "Marly and I are off job hunting. Maybe you guys should stick a little closer to the house today, okay? And tell Curtis I'll see if I can recover his flashlight after I get home this afternoon. We shouldn't be near as late today."

"Sure," said Matt. "Good luck."

"You, too." Marly looked tense and anxious in her job-hunting clothes. She hadn't often looked that way since they'd left Wichita; and even so, she didn't look near as tense as Jessy had been used to seeing her. Even worried, she was more comfortable in San Antonio.

By the time they had walked out the front door—Goldie calling, "By good-bye" as if she were proud of herself for being able to—Jessy had control of her mouth. "Cross-stitch," she said, so slowly and carefully she didn't stutter at all.

It was a shame Matt was so ignorant. "What's cross-stitch?"

Jessy rolled her eyes impatiently. "On s-sampler."

"You mean—more clues on the map? *X* marks the spot! Let's go check!"

He beat her to her room, but it didn't help him. "The only *x*'s on the map sampler are the ones making the letters," he complained. "The map is all made with other kinds of stitches. There sure aren't any *x*'s on the creek."

Jessy stood on the bed for a closer look, but couldn't find anything either. And it had been such a good idea, too! She was still trying to make it work when the phone rang, and Matt ran downstairs to answer it. She had strayed on to the other samplers, trying to twist their words around into clues—if talk was gold, silence was silver; but that didn't help—when he galloped back. "Curtis is on his way over," he said. "He didn't think much of Goldie's clues at first, but then he thought maybe 'cross creek' meant a cross on the creek—not the map creek, the real one. Like on a tree trunk or a rock."

Jessy didn't feel much like having Curtis come back after the way he'd bugged her about getting scared; but it was a good idea, and she didn't want to get left out. She had been wearing shorts to keep from chafing her scrapes, but one of the new rules was that jeans must be worn while treasure hunting, so she taped gauze pads to her thighs and changed.

On being told of Daddy's promise to get the flashlight back, Curtis cheered up some. "I thought that bit with the parrot was kind of dumb at first," he told Jessy, as he laid out his map and marked the places they should search. "But the more I think about it, the better I like it. Mr. Holz used to talk about the treasure and the bird at the same time a lot."

"And it's hard to think of another good reason to teach her to say things like 'cross creek,'" put in Matt.

"Yeah. You know, if you opened your mouth more, Jessy, and let some of the stuff in your head come out where folks could get at it, some people might get to thinking you're smart."

Jessy shrugged.

"What's this note at the bottom of the legal pad, squirt?" asked Matt. "'Who owns the money if it's found where?'"

Jessy licked her lips, talking slowly. "Gr-great-Aunt Lucy got the m-money."

"Oh, you afraid it might be hers even if we find it?" asked Curtis. "Don't worry about that. They tell you this stuff in the *Treasure-Hunters' Digest*. Money belongs to whoever owns the land it's on. That's why I got that signed agreement from your mom. If you don't have a signed agreement, it doesn't matter what they told you or how hard you worked; the owner can keep it all. I'm real glad Goldie said that bit about 'never sold,' you know. I was beginning to be scared the treasure was on the apartment side, and the owner won't give me a signed agreement. I tried."

"We can't look that far away," said Matt, pointing to one of the places Curtis had marked. "Tad-the-Dad said to stay close to the house today."

Curtis made an impatient noise. "Do you always do what your folks tell you to?"

"Mostly," said Matt. "You've got to follow the chain of command."

"I bet your dad the leatherneck told you that."

"Yeah, and he's right, too. You think they'd let us go treasure hunting if they didn't know they could trust me? Life's a lot easier if you let the grown-ups know you know they're boss."

"My dad says—" began Curtis; but Jessy was bored. She patted the map. "Wh-where do we st-start?"

Matt and Curtis agreed that there was no point in looking for *x*'s in the creekbed, since they had explored all the area near the house thoroughly, so they set up a search pattern that covered the upper bank and all the trees within about ten feet of the water. Matt thought they could eliminate all the short trees, since the robbery had happened so long ago, but Curtis pointed out that Great-Uncle Matthew might have put the *x* down himself to help him find the treasure again. Curtis's theory of why he hadn't gotten the treasure himself was that Great-Uncle Matthew had only found it during the last couple of years, since selling the back pastures to the developer, and he had been saving it against an emergency.

"It'd been safe all this time," Curtis pointed out, as they loaded their thermos bottles with ice water. "Why mess with it till you need it? If he'd dug it up it'd be in all the papers and he'd have to cough up the taxes, and people'd be bugging him to contribute to saving the whales and stuff."

"He could've fixed up the house, though," said Matt. "Mom says we've got to put in new plumbing if we stay, and the chimney's about to come down. Why didn't he take care of that?"

"Maybe he meant to and kept putting it off. Okay if we split up? It'll go faster. How'll Jessy let us know she found something?"

"You can whistle as good as anybody, can't you?" said Matt.

Jessy nodded.

"Oh, and Jess," he said, sounding as superior as if he weren't just repeating what Curtis and Marly had told him, "there are snakes around, but mostly they aren't poisonous. If it's got a triangular head it's a water moccasin, and you leave it alone; but they mostly come out at night so I wouldn't worry about it."

"Don't forget to tell her about the scorpions and the tarantulas." Curtis grinned.

Jessy stuck her nose in the air.

"Oh, she knows what they look like," said Matt.

Jessy hadn't realized what hard work treasure hunting was. Her eyes soon ached from looking for x's on tree bark or on the frequent outcrops of cementlike rock. Many of the little trees she picked her way among had long thorns that caught at her. The sky was brilliant blue, cloudless, and hot as it always was in San Antonio, which meant that she was soon dripping with sweat. She didn't meet any scorpions or tarantulas, but they would have made a nice change from mosquitoes. The Kansas City Royals cap Matt had loaned her made the backs of her ears ache and her forehead itch, but at least it kept the sun out of her eyes—Matt, of course, wore his USMC cap, and Curtis had a black-and-white one that said SPURS. She was examining the area farthest out from the creek, certain that the boys had given it to her because it was the least likely place for the treasure to be.

Curtis examined all the big trees and rock outcrops on the edge of the creekbed, and Matt had the middle section; both of which, Jessy thought crossly, were shadier than where she was. Only Clyde really seemed to enjoy himself. He startled a jackrabbit and chased it, tried to dig up a burrow, which Curtis said, on the basis of tracks, must be an armadillo's, and ran back and forth with his tongue hanging out, looking happy.

Jessy was beginning to get hungry when she found the old corral. She had been looking straight at it for at least a minute before she recognized what it was. Now it was only a ring of posts, mostly falling down, with tangles of mesquite, Queen Anne's lace (turned to burs now), and palo verde instead of barbed wire blocking the space between the posts. It was only a few feet from the path to the ford, on the edge of the search area.

Jessy didn't think the corral would be a very good place to hide treasure, but she was tired of looking for x's anyway. The gateposts were the thickest and tallest part of the corral remaining, but the gate had fallen to bits, leaving scraps of gray timber, reddish brown hinges, and rust marks on the posts as its only remains. Jessy waded into Queen Anne's lace as high as her neck, hundreds of fuzzy burrs snagging her jeans, shirt, and the hairs on her arms. She was just thinking that exploring the corral wasn't worth it, when she saw the gray shape standing rigid in the middle.

A cross shape.

10/ Disappointment

JESSY SHOVED aside the Queen Anne's lace and pushed her way through to the cross. A long piece of old, half-rotted wood had been stuck into the ground with a shorter crossbar nailed on. It leaned to one side, as if it were tired, and woodpeckers or termites had riddled the wood with holes, but it was still a cross.

Jessy found that she was shaking all over. She still didn't know what "ghost bank" or "gay tank" meant, but this was a cross by the creek, all right! Wait'll Matt saw this! She whistled; but her dry mouth made hardly any sound. After two or three tries and several deep breaths she managed a wordless scream, which she found she could draw out and out and out by leaving her mouth open and vibrating her vocal cords until she ran out of breath.

By that time the boys and Clyde were crashing toward her, Clyde barking and Matt calling, "Jessy! Jessy, what is it?" She was surprised at how scared they looked; but she was too busy pointing proudly at the cross to care. Matt's expression changed to anger.

"Cripes, don't scare me like that! I thought you'd sat in a wasp's nest at least!"

"Don't knock it," said Curtis. "She's found it!"

Matt seemed to see the cross for the first time. "Well, what do you know?" He walked all around it, tramping down the Queen Anne's lace, then examined it more closely. "It's been here a while. Look, the nails are rusty." He looked at Curtis, his eyes all shiny. "I bet you're right, though. You couldn't leave this in the middle of a working corral. I bet Great-Uncle Matthew put it here during the last few years. I wonder how he found it?"

"Never mind all that. Where's the shovels?"

The shiny look went out of Matt's face, and he kicked the ground with his heel. "Rats. I promised Mom not to dig anywhere without permission. We'll have to wait till they get home."

"Oh, come off it," moaned Curtis. "The treasure's right there! You know it's got to be. What's she going to do to you? Break your knees? Believe me, when she sees all the gold, she'll forget all about any little broken promises."

"It doesn't matter what she'd do to me. You don't break promises. You promised, too, Curt—in the signed agreement."

Jessy was with Curtis on this one. "Sh-she w-won't c-care!"

"Look, maybe people in y'all's families break promises, but we don't in mine!" Matt folded his arms, looking as stern and grim as the picture of his dad in Marine dress uniform that Matt kept on his dresser. "You know, one time Great-Uncle Matthew promised my grandad—his little brother—that he'd be somewhere at a certain time, and his car broke down, so he got up at four in the morning and walked ten miles to the bus, because the bus lines didn't come out here then, and he got where he was supposed to be half an hour early. He never even thought of calling grandad and saying, 'Look, my car doesn't work and I can't make it.' That's how we keep promises in my family!"

Jessy and Curtis both tried, but there wasn't any budging him, so they went home and ate peanut butter-and-banana sandwiches. Goldie got one, too, as a reward, and they sat around the screen porch discussing what to do with their money. Matt and Jessy, of course, would get to stay in San Antonio, but even after paying taxes and fixing up the house there would probably be lots left over. Matt wanted an IBM computer—"Marly and Tad-the-Dad could use it, too; and there's all kinds of games you can play on an IBM."—while Jessy's only indecision was whether to get an Arabian mare or a Tennesse Walking horse. Curtis's quarter share wouldn't stretch as far, but he was sure he could buy a house big enough for his whole family, including his grandmother, in a really good neighborhood, and invest the rest. By the time he graduated he'd have enough money to treasure hunt full time. "Most people just fool around with it," he said. "I mean, maybe they put their whole lives into it, but they never find any treasure, and it's not because there's no treasure out there. It's because they aren't using their heads. But me, I'll be a professional. Did you ever hear of the Lost Bowie Mine? I got a theory about that."

When Daddy and Marly drove up, they all ran out to the car talking at once—even Jessy, who couldn't get much past "I f-f-f-found." Clyde was as excited as if he understood what was going on, and barked louder than anybody could speak. It wasn't any wonder, really, that in all that babble the only thing the grown-ups noticed was the number of burs on the kids' clothes and hair.

"Where on earth did these come from?" demanded Marly, trying to brush off Jessy's T-shirt.

"I thought I told you to stay close to the house," said Daddy.

"We did!" said Matt. "We got a new clue and—"

"Jessy did it," Curtis said, interrupting, "but we were all looking—"

"G-g-goldie kn-kn-knew," said Jessy.

Daddy held up his hands. "One at a time!" he thundered, in a classroom voice, and they all fell silent, even Clyde. "Okay," he said. "We're pretty tired, so let's go have a Coke and Matt can tell us what's going on."

"Oh, man," moaned Curtis; but they all did as Daddy said. Matt tried to keep the recital short, but they made him go back and explain about Goldie's clues. Daddy had a hard time with them. "Was your great-uncle really that, um, complicated in his thinking?" he asked.

"Actually, it sounds a little like him," said Marly. "Though you'd think even he would've said straight out to somebody, 'I know where there's buried treasure and I'm going to leave clues for people to hunt for it.'"

When she actually heard the description of the cross, however, she shook her head. "Oh, you poor things. I wish I'd been here when you found it!"

Poor things? Jessy looked at Marly anxiously.

"What's the matter?" asked Matt. "Do you know something about that cross?"

"I should," said Marly. "Cousin Howard and Rachel and I put it up."

Jessy felt like a deflated balloon.

"What for?" asked Curtis.

"It's a grave marker," said Marly. "Great-Uncle Matthew used to have this beautiful collie named Tippie. One day when we were all visiting, Rachel and I were playing by the woodpile, and Tippie knocked us down. We were mad, but then we saw she had this big black spider in her mouth, and what she'd done was—I don't know how she knew to do this, but she was an awful smart dog—she'd seen we were about to get into a black widow's nest and she shoved us away and snapped at the spider."

"That wasn't too bright," said Curtis.

"You can only ask so much from a dog," said Marly. "Anyway, she got bit, and we took her to the vet, but he was out dealing with somebody's sick cow or something and his assistant was an idiot and poor Tippie died before we could get any decent help for her. But we kids decided she was a heroine and deserved a heroic burial, so we took her out to the corral, which wasn't being used anymore, and we put up a cross on her grave and sang 'Shall We Gather at the River.' " Marly blinked, looking as if it still made her sad to think of Tippie dying for her sake. Jessy felt kind of lumpy in her throat herself. "We even put her name and the date on it, and something about heroic dogs, but that was all in black tempera paint and I guess it wore off. I'm sorry, y'all."

Matt stirred. "You told me that story," he said. "You even said it was in Great-Uncle Matthew's corral. Only I didn't make the connection."

Everybody was quiet for a minute; then Curtis rinsed his Coke can and threw it in the recycling bin. "Well. That was a bust. But we can look again tomorrow. And if we find another cross, we'll see if we can make the rest of the clues fit, too."

"Have you got any idea what 'gay tank' means?" asked Matt hopefully.

Marly shook her head, blinking some more. "This is awfully hard on you kids, isn't it?" she said. "It's as if you're not getting any vacation at all. Tell you what, let's all take this Saturday off and go downtown. Tad and Jessy haven't even seen the Alamo yet, and I understand they've done a lot of things to downtown since I was here last—a Vietnam memorial, and a big mall, and lots of things." She smiled one of her brave smiles. "I want you to see something of my hometown."

Daddy scooted back his chair. "That sounds like a good idea. Curtis, let me get my clothes changed, and we'll go see if we can retrieve your flashlight."

Two disappointments in two days left Jessy feeling hollow and tired; but she got up the next morning, and the next, to look for crosses on the creek, ghost banks, and gay tanks, whatever those were. Daddy and Marly didn't find jobs, though Marly's cousin Rachel had a friend with a decorating firm where somebody would be leaving soon on maternity leave, and Marly might be able to take her place for a while. This didn't make Jessy feel much better. If only one of them found work, it needed to be Daddy.

It was funny how going back to Wichita had gotten to be a dreadful idea. It wasn't like Wichita was a bad place or anything; but the longer Jessy lived in the old farmhouse, with Clyde and the kittens (Marly had allowed some of the younger cats to come inside, and one of them liked to sleep on Jessy's bed), and the stables across the road where she could go look at horses anytime she felt like it (though treasure hunting didn't leave much time for that), turtles in the creek and jackrabbits and mocking-birds and doves, and the pear tree by the garage getting heavier and heavier as the pears grew—the worse every-thing about leaving seemed.

When Marly took them downtown on Saturday, she showed them a river the banks of which were kept partly like a shopping center and partly like a park. If you followed it south of downtown there was a neighborhood of old fancy houses surrounded by poorer sections and businesses that was like walking into another world. Maybe there were places like that in Wichita, but Jessy had never seen them. She was beginning to see why Marly loved this city so much.

The trip downtown—and the trips to the old Spanish missions and the water park in the nearby town of New Braunfels that Marly took them on later—should have been lots of fun. Matt and Jessy did enjoy them, once they got going; but they used up so much time! July was getting away from them. Soon, very soon now, Daddy would have to make up his mind whether he was going back to teach school in Wichita this fall; and if nothing changed, his mind would be made up for him.

The room he and Marly had moved into was the front one on the same side as Jessy's, separated from Matt's by the width of the stairs coming into the hall. Jessy was almost always wakened by the racket the ancient plumb-ing made when they showered.

On the last night of July, she lay in bed, sore and exhausted, too hot even to touch the kitten stretched beside her feet. She had been treasure hunting all day, climbing around a rocky place that she and Matt and Curtis had agreed might count as a ghost bank; but there had been no crosses, and she had broken one of her fingernails down into the fleshy part of her finger, what Daddy called the quick. The finger still throbbed; and she was worried about her clothes. Her jeans had a hole in them, and she was afraid she had started growing. She didn't want Marly and Daddy to have to pay for new clothes for her. She didn't want Marly to think she was expensive.

Daddy and Marly were taking an awfully long time to get to bed. The pipes rattled and banged in the walls; footsteps went back and forth in the hall; and they kept talking, in voices too low to make sense, even after all the lights were out and they should have been safely in bed.

The voices were low; but they also sounded angry. Jessy lay with her stomach tied into knots for as long as she could stand it, then got up and put her ear to the wall. It didn't help much—the walls were pretty thick—but she could hear some words.

". . . willing to move all over the world with that marine . . ." said Daddy.

A while later Marly wailed, "I hate Wichita!"

Crying was mixed with the voices for a while, then Marly said, in what would have been a shout if she hadn't been so careful to be quiet, ". . . can't be helped! Don't you see that?"

"I don't see anything!"

Jessy couldn't stand to listen, but she couldn't stand not listening either. Her ears were ringing, her eyes were blurring, and her throat was sore with tears. She went into the bathroom and cried, blowing her nose on toilet paper and then washing her face in cold water; only it never got very cold. When she came out again, she was surprised to see Matt, in his pajama bottoms, sitting at the top of the stairs. He leaned his back against the banister and looked at her. She stared back. What was Matt, the super-well-behaved one, doing up after bedtime?

All was quiet from Daddy and Marly's room now. Matt beckoned her over and led her into his room. The fan there was old and noisy, covering up the sound of his voice so that even Jessy, right next to him, could barely hear him. "You heard them fighting, didn't you?" he said.

Jessy nodded.

"Did you hear what about?"

"Wh-where to live," said Jessy, surprised at the ease with which this came out of her throat. She didn't feel tight anymore; just empty.

"Dad and Mom used to fight at night all the time," said Matt. "The last year. Before he went overseas. I guess you were too little to remember how it was before your mom left, huh?"

Jessy nodded again.

"You shouldn't worry about it," said Matt in his kindest voice. "It's got nothing to do with us, you know. I mean—it would be just the same if we weren't here."

Jessy didn't believe that; and she was tired to death. "You d-don't have t-to b-be so"—she paused and took a careful breath, miraculously spitting out the unnecessary word without hesitation—"dadgum n-nice to me."

"Cripes," muttered Matt. "There's no pleasing some people." His voice sounded kind of raggedy.

Jessy thought she should say something, but she couldn't think what it should be.

"Go on and sulk then," he said, sounding even more ragged, as if he couldn't tell if he were angry or sad. "It won't do any good. Maybe even finding the treasure won't, but we've got to try. Unless you'd rather go back to the way things were before. Maybe you would like that."

Jessy shook her head. "I d-don't sulk."

"You do too," said Matt. "I know you've had it worse than me. You don't have to rub it in all the time. At least nobody's going to shoot at your mom in that commune." He stopped, then climbed onto his bed under the big side windows. "Go to bed."

Not knowing what else to do, Jessy did.

11 / Deadline

THE NEXT MORNING everyone tried to act as if nothing had happened. Nobody succeeded, and nobody commented on anybody else's lack of success. They ate yogurt and cold cereal because Marly said it was too hot to cook; but she cut up big Mexican strawberries to put in the corn flakes, which was all the cereal they had. Before Marly came along, Jessy and Daddy had always had three or four different kinds of cereal on hand.

Jessy ate her corn flakes, remembering. What did she care if Daddy and Marly stayed together, anyway? Without her they could eat cereal with marshmallow bits again—

Instead of pancakes and bacon, omelettes, hash browns and eggs, spicy raisin oatmeal, biscuits and gravy.

They could sleep till all hours in the summer—

And eat in a dark, tiny kitchen or in the living room in front of the TV, instead of talking about their plans for the day with sunshine on the floor and a kitten rubbing against her foot.

Nobody would make her talk when she didn't want to.

She used to go days and days without saying a word at home—

Feeling small and lonesome the whole time. And Daddy—she had never thought about this before, but the memory was suddenly vivid—used to come home tired out and get up in the morning to make his old joke about how maybe he should just photocopy his days so he didn't have to keep going through them time after time after time. He hadn't made that joke once since he'd married Marly; and even when he was tired, he would look at her and smile.

"I'm going to go ahead and have a real estate agent come out today or tomorrow," said Marly, with carefully faked casualness.

"Aw, Mom," moaned Matt. "We've still got two whole weeks."

"And we've got to be realistic," said Marly. "The odds of either of us finding a job in the time left are almost nil, let alone both of us. I'm sorry, Matt."

Jessy's stomach hurt, but she made herself eat all her cereal. So the fight last night had not ended with Marly deciding to stay here alone with Matt. That was good as far as it went; but she couldn't get the sound of Marly's voice crying, "I hate Wichita!" out of her head. After breakfast she ran straight upstairs and brushed her teeth and made her bed, not waiting for Marly to remind her.

She and Matt both hunted extra hard for the treasure that day, and the next, which was the day the real estate agent came. When they came in for supper Marly was extra busy, hanging out clothes—she usually washed clothes and hung them out in the mornings before going job hunting so they would be dry when she got home—

and smiling her bravest smile. The house smelled of chicken fricassee.

Daddy was the one who delivered the bad news. "The real estate agent doesn't think we can sell except to developers. It's always possible to get lucky if we hold out, of course. There are people that really like this kind of house, but they're mostly buying in the historic districts farther into town; and there are people who really like this sort of property, but they're mostly buying farther out into the country because they don't want everything around them to be built up."

"And if we hold out too long we'll have to pay too many taxes and might as well not have tried to sell anyway," said Matt.

Daddy nodded.

"Look, we all knew life was imperfect," said Marly, as if she were angry. "Every single person at this table has good reason to know that you can't always get what you want or keep what you have. Sometimes you have to settle for second best."

"Sometimes," said Daddy.

Second best, thought Jessy. That's us.

There was a lot of chicken fricassee left over that night.

Jessy and Matt and Curtis had searched the whole creek up to the property lines on each side, and had not found any other crosses. Not one. So what did that leave? Jessy felt like she'd spent the whole summer crawling through brush and cactus, sweating and mosquito-bit, not spending any time to really enjoy all the things there were to enjoy, the stables and the turtles and Goldie and the kittens—and for what? They'd never find the treasure. Great-Uncle Matthew's clues were too devious. The only reason she could think of for not giving up was so that Matt's opinion of her wouldn't get even lower, and she didn't know why she cared about that; but she wasn't a sulker and she wouldn't quit.

Only she couldn't think what else they could do, and neither Matt nor Curtis was doing any better.

The day after the real estate agent came, Daddy got a temporary job from an agency. It wasn't much of a job, but he said there was a possibility of it becoming permanent, so he took it. Marly dropped him off and went job hunting, leaving Matt and Jessy to their own devices, as usual.

Only today they didn't seem to have any devices. A visit to Great-Aunt Lucy in the morning, to extract more information, was not helpful. She told them the story of the money again, fed them chess pie, and sympathized. "I'd loan you the money for taxes," she said. "It would leave me a little tight in the budget, but I'd do it. Only Marly says it wouldn't do any good, because the house should be fixed up before winter, and what if I broke my hip or something?"

"How'd your daddy pay off whatever money he needed to borrow that time he couldn't get a loan from Lamar?" asked Curtis.

Great-Aunt Lucy shrugged. "Land, I don't know! I was younger than Jessy is now and barely knew there was a crisis. I remember when the bank man came, though— can you believe he came all the way out here to collect? I think he was going to foreclose. And Daddy counted out the money in gold, right there on the kitchen table, the exact right amount and shoved it toward him and said, 'There it is. You don't want to know what I went through to get it on time.' And the bank man said, 'You're right,' picked up his hat and his money, and left."

Curtis was quiet the rest of the visit and all the way back to the ford. "We missed something," he said, stepping from stone to stone. "We must have."

"M-maybe G-goldie knows some m-more cl-clues," suggested Jessy, not very hopefully.

"I wish she could talk more clearly," complained Matt. "Sometimes you have to already know what she's saying before you can understand her. Like, she really says 'gretty gatthew,' but you know she means 'pretty Matthew.' Maybe she's saying 'pay bank' instead of 'gay tank.' How would we know?"

"How would it help?" asked Curtis.

Jessy stopped, as she often did now, at the corral to look at Tippie's grave. It was terrible to think of a bull-dozer crashing through the posts, knocking down the cross, scooping up the remains of the heroic dog, and putting a parking lot or a sidewalk or a streetlamp where she had been. And what would happen to the cats? And Clyde? You couldn't move an unhousebroken dog to the city.

They got themselves iced tea and went to the screen porch, for lack of better ideas. Goldie jingled her bells at them—she had almost chewed through the leather strap—and said cheerfully, "Hello, hello! Goldie is a treasure bird."

"Goldie is a chicken dinner if she doesn't cough up some better clues," said Curtis.

Jessy glared at him; but Curtis didn't understand glares. "D-don't b-be mean," she said. "She's d-doing the b-best she c-can."

"Who's being mean?" Curtis sat on the floor with his back against the screen door. "Come on, Goldie. Treasure bird. Where's the treasure, bird?"

"Treasure bird," said Goldie, jingling the bells and then imitating their sound. "Talk is gold, never sold. Talk is gold. Never sold."

"Hey, Mom's back already," said Matt, pointing through the screen at the driveway.

Marly parked outside the garage and came up the sidewalk to the side porch, her business outfit, her hair, and her shoulders all looking limp and defeated. "No leads today," said Curtis knowledgeably. "That's the way my dad looks when he can't even find a place to apply."

"D-does that happen a l-lot?" asked Jessy.

Curtis nodded. "Yeah. That's why I'm so big on finding treasure, you know? You can't depend on other people to keep you employed. The only person you can depend on is yourself." He stood up and opened the screen door.

Marly had been looking at the sidewalk and didn't see them till then. First she looked surprised, then she stood up straight and put on her brave, cheerful face. "Hello, Curtis," she said. "How are you today?"

"Fine, ma'am," said Curtis.

"Good morning," said Goldie, hanging upside down from her cage. "Gold morning. Goldie is a treasure bird."

"You're home awfully early," said Matt.

It made Jessy's face ache to see the way Marly kept her face cheerful. "I seem to have come to the end of my resources, so I figured I'd come home and get some housework done. Y'all taking a break from treasure hunting?"

"We're kind of at the end of our resources, too," said Matt.

"How d-do you g-get G-goldie to say what you w-want?" asked Jessy. She didn't really think Marly would be any help; but if they all went back to Wichita, there'd be no use cleaning a house that was just going to be torn down; and if Daddy and Marly split up, she wanted them to do things together while they could.

"Well, you have to get her to think of the words," she said. "You can teach her to respond to certain questions. Like"—a genuine smile replaced the determined one—"where's the bathroom?"

"Ugstairs, enda the hall," said Goldie, and whistled.

The children laughed. "I never heard her say that before!" said Matt.

"You never asked the right question. When I brought your dad here the first time, he asked me that, and Goldie piped up and answered. I thought he'd die."

"I've tried asking, 'Where's the treasure?' " said Curtis. "That doesn't work."

"It doesn't have to be a question. Let me see your list of clues."

Jessy gave her the legal pad and slid out of the recliner so Marly could sit down. Marly slipped off her high-heeled sandals and studied the list. "That's interesting," she said. "You've got two rhyming couplets. Have you noticed that?"

"Two whats?" asked Matt.

"Couplets. When two lines right next to each other in poetry rhyme, that's a couplet. Not that you could call this poetry. 'Gay tank' rhymes with 'ghost bank,' whatever they mean; and 'talk is gold' rhymes with 'never sold.' I guess you hadn't noticed because 'talk is gold' is in the second column."

Jessy felt as if two jigsaw puzzle pieces that had looked nothing alike had suddenly come together. "Gr-great-Aunt Lucy said-d he tr-tried to t-teach her p-poetry."

"So the clues make a poem?" Curtis turned to Goldie. "Okay, bird, what's the rhyme for creek? Cross creek, cross creek."

"Cross creek, corral seek," Goldie said.

"But we've been to the corral," said Curtis.

"Treasure bird," suggested Matt, looking at the second column. "Goldie is a treasure bird."

"Cross creek, corral seek, Goldie is a treasure bird."

"Oh," said Marly, her face suddenly still and shiny. "Corral seek by the crossing of the creek. That's what she means. It was all grown over and Great-Uncle Matthew was afraid we wouldn't find it. Maybe he even meant Tippie's grave to bring us to the corral. Oh, drat the man! Why couldn't he ever say anything straight?"

Marly believed in the treasure now, Jessy realized. Five minutes ago she hadn't really, and now she did. The difference it made in her face was amazing.

"But where are we supposed to dig in the corral?" asked Matt.

"Was there ever a stock tank in there?" asked Curtis.

"Just a trough." Marly stood up. "Let me go get changed."

"Ch-changed for what?" asked Jessy, but she knew the answer.

"Changed for treasure hunting," said Marly. "We're going to find that sucker."

12 / Corral

IN A QUARTER of an hour they were heading for the corral, everybody, including Marly, in jeans, T-shirts, and baseball caps—Marly's was orange and had a longhorn cow's face on it; she had owned it ever since she went to school at the University of Texas at Austin—and carrying tools. Jessy almost laughed everytime she looked at Marly; she looked so funny with her hair tucked up, a garden fork in one hand, and Goldie riding on her work glove.

Goldie flapped her wings, stretched her head to look at everything they passed, and might have flown off a couple of times except for the leash Marly had clipped to Goldie's leg, with the other end clipped to her watchband. "Corral seek!" Goldie squawked. "Goldie is a treasure bird! Jingle jingle!" Clyde danced around barking, and Goldie barked back.

At the corral, Marly found a sturdy hackberry branch and clipped Goldie to it. "Now," she said, taking the swingblade, "we've all got to try and think like Great-Uncle Matthew. All the clues should make sense if you look at them right, and they must have something to do with the corral—something that only makes sense here, or you can only see from here, something. Stand back while I clear these weeds. Clyde, sit!"

Clyde sat, wagging his tail and grinning. "Matt and I can do that," offered Curtis, but Marly shook her head.

"I think better when I'm working. Let's go through the clues one at a time."

"Talk is gold," said Goldie, walking up and down on her branch and trying to see everything around her at once.

" 'Talk is gold' means that the parrot's talk will lead us to the gold," said Curtis, "and 'never sold' means we don't have to worry about the land he sold off to make expenses."

Jessy stood by the hackberry, trying to think and not succeeding very well.

"And 'cross creek' means the ford," said Matt, leaning on the gatepost and pointing down the path, "and maybe Tippie's grave. You sure it's no good digging there, Mom?"

Dust and a smell like old, dry carrot tops rose around Marly as she hacked through the weeds. "I'm sure," said Marly. "We dug that grave deep and wide. Besides, the middle of a corral is a lousy place to bury treasure. Any marks you left to tell yourself where to dig would be obliterated by a thousand tramping hooves."

The corral was much bigger around than the two-car garage, and all the posts were the same size, except for the two at the gate.

"Cross creek, corral seek," said Matt. "But—"

"Cross creek, corral seek," said Goldie, sitting as far

out on the branch as her leash would let her go, stretching her neck out and leaning forward. "Ghost bank. Gayt ank."

"Where was the trough?" asked Curtis. "If he said 'cross' instead of 'ford,' maybe he said 'tank' instead of 'trough.'"

"That's an idea," said Marly, wiping her forehead. "Actually, there were three or four; but Great-Uncle Matthew hauled them off for scrap metal ages ago. I doubt I could locate them anymore."

"Gretty Gatthew," said Goldie.

Suddenly Jessy realized that they had all been holding one of their jigsaw pieces upside down. "P-p-p—" Drat her mouth!

"Slow down, Jess," said Matt.

Everyone was looking at her, even Goldie and Clyde. She took a deep breath and said the clue in two parts, carefully, without hesitation. "Post. Bank."

"Post bank," agreed Goldie; and Jessy could see from their faces that they all heard her correctly this time.

"Post bank," said Marly. She stopped swinging the blade. "A fence-post bank. Oh, how stinking obvious!" She looked around the corral. "All we need to know is which post, and the last clue—Come on, Goldie. Say it again. Post bank. Post bank."

"Post bank, gaytyank," said Goldie.

"Gay tank," repeated Curtis. "Gay tank."

Goldie stood up to her full height and stretched her wings. "Gate yank!"

Suddenly Jessy understood, and she could see Curtis understanding at the same time. She laughed and clapped her hands. "Gate yank!" shouted Curtis. "Yank it up!"

Marly laughed, too. Matt continued looking blank, until she ran over to him and slapped the post he was leaning on. "Yank up the gate post!" she said. "It's a fence-post bank that we need to yank up before we can find the money! Oh, if Great-Uncle Matthew were alive, I'd strangle him!"

Light finally dawned on Matt's face, too. "But—that must've been a heck of a chore," he said. "It's such a big post, and you'd have had to yank up the whole gate, too, when it was new."

"You're right . . . so it must be . . . yes." She turned to the other post, where the gate latch would have been. "This is the one. Give me a hand, guys."

They all clustered round, loosening the earth around the post with the garden fork and the spade, then wiggling it back and forth—like wiggling a tooth, Jessy thought. The ground was hard and dry, and soon they all had sweat running down their faces. "I think we can get it out now," panted Marly. "But remember, even now we could be wrong. Or Lamar's treasure could be exaggerated, all worthless paper money or something. Or—"

"Quit it, Mom," said Matt. "We all know it can still go bust. Why not find out?"

Marly smiled nervously. "Okay. You're right. Now, everybody take hold—one set of hands above the other—and when I say the word we'll all pull up at the same time. Ready? One, two, three, go!"

Jessy was at the bottom, with Matt's hands above hers and Curtis straining beside her. The post came up, up, straight up. It was heavier than she had expected, but

114 /

with so many hands helping her hold it, it couldn't fall back down. They laid it neatly aside. Jessy, being the closest to the ground, was the first to look in the hole; but it was too dark to see anything. She reached in, and her hand met soft, crumbly dirt, with something hard underneath. Curious, Clyde pushed his nose in next to her face. "Th-there's something," she said.

"We'll have to widen the hole a bit," said Marly, picking up the fork as Matt hauled Clyde back.

Jessy stood on one foot, then on the other. Matt hung onto Clyde's collar, and Curtis cracked his knuckles, passing Marly the spade when she asked for it. Goldie chattered away unheeded, talking about corrals and treasure birds and pretty Matthew, whistling and croaking at the grackles who lighted in the next tree to inspect her. The hole got wider, but not much deeper, dirt falling down from the sides as fast as Marly could scoop it off the top. At last she put down the spade and reached into the hole, seeming to brush something away.

"Great goshamighty," she said. "I didn't think they made mason jars this size."

The children crowded around. All Jessy could see was a jar lid sticking out of the dirt, its gold color speckled with black tarnish. Marly, lying on her stomach, placed both gloved hands on its rim. "I'm almost afraid to open it."

"Don't be a wimp, Mom," said Matt.

"I'm afraid for you not to open it," said Curtis. "I'm afraid if you don't open it we'll all bust."

Marly laughed nervously, and twisted. The lid turned grudgingly, with a grating noise. The rim came up in her hand, leaving the center part of the lid still covering the jar's mouth. Matt reached in and pried at the edge with the file on his Swiss Army knife, and it popped up.

Inside was a white envelope, folded small and tight. Marly lifted it, revealing another envelope, thick and yellow and folded, tied together with string. Marly lifted that.

The jar was three-quarters full of small yellow coins.

Jessy squealed and clapped her hands. Matt and Curtis cheered. Clyde barked. Goldie shouted and clapped her wings, scaring the grackles. Only Marly was quiet, reaching into the jar and pulling out a handful, and then another. "It's real," she said. "It's really real."

All kinds of gold coins were mixed up together: one, and two-and-a-half, and three, and five, and ten, and twenty-dollar coins, with Indian heads and crowned women, with eagles flying or standing or holding flag-covered shields. They were smaller than Jessy had expected, less than an inch across; but they were bright and yellow and glinted in the sun. No wonder Lamar had liked them, she thought, turning over a twenty-dollar gold piece with an eagle flying across the sun on one side and a tall robed lady waving a branch and a staff on the other. This was better than paper money. This was round and solid in your hand, good to feel, gorgeous to look at.

"We've got to tell Tad," said Marly. "We've got to tell Great-Aunt Lucy."

"We've got to take it away and count it," said Curtis.

"How are we going to get it out?" asked Matt. "There must be a hundred pounds of gold here."

"Not quite that much, but it'll be hard to lift the whole jar. We'll rebury it and come back with some help," said

Marly. "Cousin Howard should have the right equipment."

Curtis shook his head. "No. What if somebody comes along?"

"Who?" asked Marly. "It's been safe this long."

"Everybody at the apartments knows Matt and I've been looking for treasure," said Curtis. "What if some kid gets bored and decides to come look, too? Maybe you're willing to risk your money, but I'm not taking any chances with my quarter share."

The thought made Jessy sick. "He's r-right," she said. "It'd b-be h-horrible to lose any of it n-now!"

Marly laughed. "Oh, don't be paranoid! Tell you what. If it bothers Curtis that much, we'll leave him to guard it. I'll call Tad and Great-Aunt Lucy and—let's see—Brandon's mother is a CPA—I'll make the calls I need to make, and Matt and Jessy can get some bags and run back and forth till all the gold's in the house. Will that satisfy you?"

All agreeing that this was the best plan, Jessy collected the two envelopes, Marly got Goldie, and all three of them carried tools. Curtis kept Clyde and the Swiss Army knife in case of danger. Once at the house, Jessy put Goldie in her cage and got her some damp carrot tops as a treat while Marly started phoning and Matt dug plastic grocery bags out of the recycling bin.

The gold was so heavy it tore the bags if they weren't careful, and the trip was a long one to make over and over again, with the weight of the treasure pulling at their shoulders and spinning around to bang against their knees, but by the time Great-Aunt Lucy came hurrying stiffly across the creek they had almost emptied the jar. She leaned against the gatepost, huffing and puffing and staring at the hole with the jar in the bottom as if she could hardly believe her eyes. "Good night!" she said. "I thought Marly'd lost her mind for sure!"

"It's true," said Matt, pulling out the last gold piece and holding it up for her. It was an old, old twenty-dollar coin, not like the ones above it—1880 according to the date under the lady's head on the front. An extraordinarily fancy eagle clutched a shield and hovered under a circle of stars on the back. "This'll be enough money to pay taxes and feed us till Mom and Tad-the-Dad find jobs, won't it? A whole jar full of this stuff?"

"I should think so! But how in the world did y'all find it? Marly didn't make much sense over the phone."

So Curtis and Matt, with Jessy happily swinging her sack beside them, occasionally nodding and laughing, told her all about it as they walked back to the house for the last time. Great-Aunt Lucy was a really satisfying audience; she kept clucking and saying, "Good night!" and, "Who would've ever thought of that?"

"We'd never ever have found it if Jessy hadn't figured that out about Goldie," said Curtis.

"I never would've put it together," said Matt, sounding a little glum. "I hardly had any good ideas this whole summer."

Was Matt actually feeling bad about not doing enough to find the treasure? That didn't seem right to Jessy. She trotted a few steps to catch up to him. "I n-never would've even tr-tried," she said. "I w-would've g-given up, b-but you never did."

"I heard that," said Curtis. "Matt here kept my nose to the grindstone all summer, too."

"You wanted to find the treasure as much as I did," said Matt.

"Yeah, but you don't know how often I wanted to blow it off for an afternoon and go swimming."

"You never said anything."

"Because you'd've kept right on working and maybe found it without me, if I had."

"I think you all did a marvelous job," declared Great-Aunt Lucy as they picked their way through the cats on the back porch.

Marly was making sandwiches and cooking chili. "Brandon's mother Shirley is on her way over, and Tad says we're the greatest family anybody could have. We're going out to eat tonight, so think about where you want to go. Can you believe this, Aunt Lucy? I keep thinking I'm going to wake up, myself." She waved her arm. Plastic grocery bags of gold were all over the table, on the porcelain pull-out counter of the Hoosier kitchen cabinet, on the drainboard, and piled on the chairs.

"Can I call my mom and dad at work?" asked Curtis, his hand on the phone by the sink.

"By all means!"

"What I can't understand," said Great-Aunt Lucy, sitting down carefully on the only chair that didn't have something stacked on it, "is why Matthew didn't tell anybody? Why go through all this trouble with Goldie and the samplers, and take such a chance on nobody ever figuring it out?"

"You s-said he had a d-devious m-mind," said Jessy.

"Yes, but even he should've known that the odds of anybody paying any attention to Goldie were terrible!"

"You know what I think?" said Marly. "I think those envelopes in Jessy's pockets will tell us all about it."

"What envelopes?" asked Great-Aunt Lucy.

Jessy had stuffed them deep into her front pockets where their bulk would be comfortable, and had to dig them out while everybody—even Curtis, who was talking to his mother—watched her. She unfolded them and laid them on the table. Marly stirred the chili. "Matt, clear our fortune off the table and chairs so we'll have someplace to eat, okay? And then we're going to finally get to the bottom of this!"

13/ Promises

MARLY PICKED up the older envelope first, opened it with her thumbnail, and unfolded the notebook papers inside. They were covered on both sides with large, round pencil-writing. "That looks like Matthew's writing," said Great-Aunt Lucy.

"It is," said Marly, checking the signature at the bottom of the last page. The paper, which had been folded into quarters and then once more lengthways, kept trying to fold up again in her hands. "It's dated twelve years ago." She took a drink of iced tea and started reading.

"To Whom It May Concern, One of My Relatives, I Hope:

"These are the gold coins my mother's uncle, Lamar Devine, hoarded under his porch during his lifetime. In 1923 his nephew-in-law, my father, Vernon Holz, had his mortgage come due and had no money to pay for it. He and I went to Uncle Lamar to ask him for a loan. Lamar had no one to leave the money to when he died but my mother, Minnie Devine

Holz, his only blood relation; if we didn't pay off the mortgage we would all be destitute; and we had always been good neighbors to him. I myself worked for him many a time with no more pay than my meals. In spite of all these considerations, Uncle Lamar refused to lend us a penny, and I was so angry I said I wished somebody would rob his precious gold from him, for he wasn't fit to have it.

"Well, I got my wish. It was that same night that somebody took that mason jar from under his porch, and of course I regretted my words. We all helped to hunt for the culprit; and my father forbade us kids from ever saying that Uncle Lamar deserved what had happened to him. The next week the mortgage man came around, and we paid off the interest in gold, but when anybody asked where it came from my father told him a man who wanted to support his family had to know how to scrape, and he had scraped."

"Wait a minute," said Curtis. "You don't think—"

"No!" said Great-Aunt Lucy sharply. "Daddy was an honest man." She took off her glasses and polished them with the edge of her shirt.

Marly, her eyes running ahead down the page, licked her lips.

"And the next two years, whenever we needed money, we would have it, sometimes just barely. My father and mother worked hard and never passed up an opportunity to earn money or teach us to do right. But one time, I went out coon hunting and came home early, there not being any coon out that my dog could tell, and I came across my father at the place where you found this. He was down on his knees reaching into the hole. I came on him unawares, and

I saw what he had down in that hole was Uncle Lamar's mason jar full of gold."

"Let me see that!" Great-Aunt Lucy snatched the papers from Marly and looked through them, her mouth screwed up tight. When she laid them down her shrunken, splotchy hands were shaking. "He d-doesn't actually say Daddy's the one that stole it," she said.

"But he knew who it belonged to," said Matt. "If he used any of it, it would still be stealing."

"He needed it, though," said Curtis. "If he was only using what he absolutely had to, when his back was against the wall and he and his wife had already worked as hard as they could and not got what they needed—" He spread his hands out, looking from Matt to Great-Aunt Lucy to Marly. "That's a little different."

"And it w-was g-going to b-be M-minnie's anyway," said Jessy.

"That must be how he thought of it," said Marly, sternly, "but everybody here knows better! Don't you?"

She fastened her eyes tight to Jessy's, and Jessy nodded.

"Yeah," said Curtis, slowly. "Shoot, poor Mr. Holz! If I found out my dad was a crook . . . I don't know what I'd do."

"What did Great-Uncle Matthew do?" asked Matt.

" 'He didn't give me any chance to ask questions,' " Marly read.

"He said, 'Matthew, I haven't done anything I wasn't forced to do; and I want you to promise you'll never tell where this is.' I didn't have time to think, and we kids were used to obeying our folks. I promised. Many's the time since then that I regretted it, but a promise is a promise. Especially to your father."

"So that explains why Great-Uncle Matthew never told anybody straight out," said Matt.

"You people and your promises," said Curtis. "It seems to me it was worse to keep quiet about stealing than it would've been to break the promise."

" 'Maybe I did right, and maybe I did wrong,' " Marly read on.

"Anyway, I've kept my promise. It wasn't too long after that that Uncle Lamar's house caught fire, and my father died of smoke inhalation, trying to get him out. The whole neighborhood knew he was a hero for that; and it would just about have broken my mother's heart to find out he was also a thief. So that was another reason to keep quiet.

"All the land hereabouts belonged to my mother after that, Uncle Lamar's and her own both, and we managed it together. Many's the time I was tempted to come out here and pull out just a little bit of all that was here; but I stood firm against the temptation, and it got easier as time went on. When the bad times really hit was in 1933, but that was the same year Franklin Delano Roosevelt passed a law against owning gold, and after that I never was tempted to dig the stuff up again."

A law against owning gold! Jessy almost panicked. "B-b-but it's ours!"

"S'okay," said Curtis. "I read all about that in the *Treasure-Hunter's Digest*. It used to be illegal to own gold except jewelry and stuff, but if you found it you turned it over to the government and they paid you for it. Then in 1974 they changed the law again, so now the gold money's legal, even if they're not making it anymore. I bet we could even spend this at the grocery store, only we'd be losing money by it."

"Go on, Mom," said Matt. "Doesn't he tell about Goldie?"

"Are you all right, Great-Aunt Lucy?" asked Marly. "Do you need a glass of water?"

Great-Aunt Lucy shook her head. "I'm fine. It's a bit of a shock, but I'm fine. Poor Matthew!"

Marly went back to the papers, laying each one aside as she finished it.

"Now they've made gold legal again; but I'm what they call an accessory after the fact. Besides, I don't want it. It's forever tainted for me. But Uncle Lamar worked hard for this money, and it does seem a shame for it never to see the light of day again. When I die, the last person who has any guilt in the matter will be gone, and it will surely be time for this gold to do some good in the world.

"I thought a long time about how to let somebody in my family know how to find this treasure without breaking my promise. It would be a terrible thing if they sold off this land to make a subdivision and the building contractor got it when they dug a foundation! A couple of years ago, one of our old hands from Mexico who went into the bird business came around, and he had this parrot. She's what you call a double-yellow-headed Amazon, and she's right smart. And I got this idea: Everybody thinks of pirates and buried treasure when they think of parrots. Why not train Goldie to be a treasure map? Why not teach her clues that will lead to this spot when I'm gone?

"I hope I did a good job and you here reading this will be someone who's been treating Goldie right and got rewarded this way. I made the clues as simple as I could, but Goldie's not good at making some noises, and I wanted to make the clues rhyme so you could tell which ones belonged and didn't get confused by her giving you directions to the bathroom or something. I hope you are somebody who will use this money to take care of your family and not waste it on fancy cars and things, but it's out of my hands. When you think about it, any way you spend it will be less of a waste than letting it sit in the ground. All anybody can do is the best he can do, and sometimes you'll be right, and sometimes you'll be wrong. Like my father, who was both."

Marly stopped reading. "That's all, except he signs it."

"Wh-what ab-bout the other env-velope?" asked Jessy.

Marly opened the newer-looking envelope. It held only one page, folded the same way. Her eyebrows went up when she unfolded it. "This begins, 'Dear Matt and Jessy, I hope.'"

"He must've written it just last year, then," said Matt.

Jessy could picture the old, awkward man in the recliner, struggling all alone with the fence post, wrestling the jar lid open, putting the envelope in for them to find. "It m-must've b-been hard w-work by then."

"He must've put it out there one day when I was off shopping," said Great-Aunt Lucy. "He'd still get active in bursts, right up till the end; but he could hardly have gone all the way to the corral and dug up that gatepost without my noticing, if I'd been around."

"Never mind that. What's he got to tell Matt and Jessy

that's so important he had to bring a whole new note for them?" asked Curtis.

Marly read:

"I expect you're wondering why I picked your part of my family to give the last chance at Uncle Lamar's gold to. Or maybe I don't expect that, and I just want to tell somebody. When you spend most of your life not telling folks things, even the folks you love best, explaining something like this gets to be a luxury you can't resist. There's all kinds of reasons. I knew it was the lack of money and a settled place to live that broke up your mom and dad's marriage, Matt—"

"That's a simplistic way of looking at it," Marly interrupted herself.

"Those were the things you always fought about," said Matt.

"And how do you know what we were fighting about?" Marly demanded. "We never fought in front of you. Never once."

"That apartment's walls were so thin, you didn't have to," said Matt. "Don't worry about it, Mom. It was a long time ago. I don't think I was traumatized. Keep reading."

Marly looked at him with an expression Jessy didn't understand; then turned her eyes back down to the page.

"I could see both of you could be quiet and well behaved enough to trust with Goldie, which none of the other kids were; and I've about figured out that the adults don't believe in the treasure enough to really hunt for it.

"Plus I had this fellow feeling for Jessy, from the minute she had such a time saying her name. It wasn't long enough ago that that was happening to me, for me to forget how that felt."

So he'd felt sorry for her, too! Jessy gritted her teeth.

"And no, Jessy, I didn't feel sorry for you. Fellow feeling's not the same."

Jessy blinked in surprise. Matt laughed. "He got your number pretty fast, squirt! You remember that next time somebody's nice to you."

Marly continued reading before Jessy had time to sort out what any of this meant.

"Lucy's always saying I have a devious mind, so I've put together some of Mama's old samplers that I hope'll give you all a hint of how to start. I've been dropping hints about the treasure everywhere. I made my will today leaving the samplers to Jessy and the parrot to Matt and the land to Marly, and what more an old man can do without breaking his promise, I don't know. I just don't.

Love, your Great-Great-Uncle Matthew Holz."

Epilogue

IN MARCH, Jessy stopped being the newest, funniest-sounding girl in her class.

Anjanette came from Boston, and people made fun of her accent on the playground. None of Jessy's friends, of course—Jessy didn't have any. Everybody had seen her and Matt on the news right before school started, and had gotten the idea they were rolling in dough. It made some people mean, and some people fake-nice. Matt had the same problem at middle school, but he at least had Curtis for company.

Jessy started to walk past the group that trailed after Anjanette, repeating her unlikely pronunciations; but then she saw the way the other girl was walking, with her head up as high as it would go and her steps getting longer and longer. How many times had she walked across playgrounds like that? Before she thought, she stepped right up to the loudest teaser and said, "Sh-she d-d-doesn't t-talk any f-f-funnier th-than I d-d-d-do." Her stutter wasn't that bad anymore, but she exaggerated it on purpose. Then she reached her hand out to Anjanette and said, "C-c-come on."

They went together to the top of the jungle gym, and Jessy tried to show her how a Texan talked. Since Jessy still sounded mostly like a Kansan with a stutter, this quickly turned into a conversation about Boston and Wichita, and how each of them came to live in Texas. Anjanette, it turned out, was there because her mother's company had moved; and she was living in the Green Pastures Apartments. "I like your house," she said. "I can see it from my window."

After school they got on the bus together. "Somebody told me you found a treasure," said Anjanette. "Is that for real?"

"Me and my br-brother and a fr-friend of his," said Jessy. "And my st-stepmom." The bus trip was not very long. She only had time to tell the shorter version.

"It's funny," said Anjanette. "Y'aaaall"—she dragged it out till Jessy was forced to laugh, at which point Anjanette smiled and went on—"don't act like rich people. If nobody told me you'd found buried treasure, I never would've thought of it."

"W-we're not rich, really," said Jessy, very slowly, as they got off the bus with the other children from the Green Pastures Apartments. The air smelled of bus fumes, but as they moved away from the street a gust of flowery air came from across the creek. Marly said March and April were the best months to be in San Antonio; and Jessy thought that smell was a big part of the reason. "Th-there was plenty of gold to p-pay taxes, and fix the house, and st-start Marly in her own business, and Curtis g-got to buy his house; b-but most of it's invested. For Matt and me to go to c-college." She took three steps, thinking. "I'm g-getting riding lessons for my b-birth-day."

"What about your dad?"

"You c-can't buy t-teaching jobs."

They cut across the grass toward Anjanette's apartment block as the other kids scattered noisily. "I wish I'd find treasure." Anjanette sighed. "Everything'd be about perfect, if Mom and Dad didn't have to worry about money, and we had a big house!"

Jessy didn't say anything. She couldn't think of anything to say that she would've believed, if she had been Anjanette. It sounded hokey to say that money didn't solve any problems except the money ones, but it was true. Jessy still stuttered, and Mommy still wasn't interested in her.

They climbed the stairs to Anjanette's door, and she took her key from around her neck. "I'd ask you to come in, but I'm not supposed to without permission," Anjanette said.

Jessy swallowed, and planned the sentence before she said it, proud to get it out with only a slight hesitation on the first word. "Wh-what about coming to our house?"

"Same thing. But when Mom gets home I'll call you and she can check you out, okay?"

Jessy nodded. "Okay."

She proceeded through the apartments, pausing at Great-Aunt Lucy's door. She used to stop in after school to eat a snack and work a jigsaw puzzle; but last month Great-Aunt Lucy had had a stroke, and she was still in the hospital learning to walk again. That was another thing the money couldn't help with. Jessy got a sick feeling in her stomach thinking about it; so she headed for the creek, thinking about spring instead.

The grass around the apartments was short and weedy, but as she got closer to the creek, bluebonnets and yellow flowers started to crop up in small, bright clumps. She picked her way across the ford, where Clyde came to meet her, and she raced him to the house between the stubby trees, breaking out in tiny bright green leaves. Bluebonnets crowded the open spaces. The pear tree by the garage was covered with white blossoms, the lilies of the valley along the back porch bloomed, and her two favorite cats waited for her. Clothes swayed on the clothesline above a half-full laundry basket. Jessy, wondering why Marly hadn't finished bringing them in, dumped her bookbag on the back porch, petted the cats, and went to the clothesline to finish pulling the clothes down; but Marly came to the door before she started.

"I thought I heard you come home," said Marly in a brave voice Jessy had not heard in some time. "Your mother's on the phone. Would you like to talk to her?"

Jessy froze with her hands on the clothespins, her cat Kaboodle rubbing against her leg. Her stomach hurt again.

"If you don't want to, I'll just tell her no," said Marly.

Jessy swallowed. "Th-that's ok-kay," she said. Still feeling sick, she went into the kitchen, where Goldie— her cage had been moved in there till the weather got warm enough to keep her on the side porch again— looked up from the twig she was demolishing and said: "Welcome home. Talk is Goldie. Pretty J-jessy!"

Her hands were wet as she picked up the phone. "H-hello?"

"Hi." The voice at the other end didn't sound the way she remembered; it was kind of thin, and weak. "How you doing?"

"F-fine." Jessy spoke very carefully. "How are you?"

"Well—" Her mother laughed nervously. "That's a pretty complicated question, really. Okay, I guess. I'm alive."

Jessy tried to think of something to say, but couldn't.

"I might not have been," said her mother's unfamiliar voice. "But that's not what I called you about. I called because, well . . . It's awfully nice of you to talk to me at all. I owe you a big apology. I, um, I know I treated you badly. And I called because I want to tell you I know that, and I'm sorry."

"Oh," said Jessy, and stopped. When somebody said she was sorry, you should say, "That's all right," but that would be a lie.

"You don't have to forgive me or anything," her mother said quickly. "I just wanted to, I needed—well, I'm in the hospital right now. I've got malnutrition. Brother Samuel's visions were, well, I was—we were all misled, and the commune's closed, and I was, I was pretty bad off for a while, but I'm all right now. And I've been talking to a priest here, Father Alvarez, and he's made me realize, realize things I never thought enough about before."

Jessy still didn't know what to say, but she had to say something. "That's g-good."

"So I'm, I'm going on this retreat next week, to get my head together and, and there were some things in my life I had to face up to. Get straight. And the biggest one is I haven't been a very good mother to you."

Jessy said nothing.

"And I'm going to, I'll do better. It's too late for a lot of things, but I will do better. I promise. But I've got to—when this retreat is over I'll call you, okay? And maybe this summer, we can get together. Okay?"

Jessy wasn't sure she wanted that, wasn't sure what she thought, but she said, "Okay."

"Okay, honey. Tell your daddy I'm glad he and, um, Marly are doing so well. Tell him I'll talk to him after the retreat, too. Okay? Bye, honey."

"Pretty J-jessy," said Goldie as she hung up. "Marly-mom. Corral seek."

Jessy sat down at the table, and Marly came in with the clothes. "So what do you think?" asked Marly.

Jessy shrugged and pressed her hands flat against the tablecloth. It was yellow, the same shade of yellow as the roses on the new wallpaper. Marly was sprucing up the whole house as she got things together to start her new interior design business. "She d-didn't even n-notice that I didn't st-stutter hardly."

Marly sat down next to her. "It sounds like she's going to try being a Catholic this time. Maybe it'll work out better for her than the communes did."

"You really th-think so?"

Marly shrugged. "We can hope."

"Wh-what's mal-nu-tri-tion?"

"Starvation. I talked to her for a while before you came home. Brother Samuel had them on some sort of weed-and-water diet, so they'd all faint and have visions. Finally, somebody ran away, and the health department raided them, or something." Marly gently pushed the hair back from Jessy's forehead.

"I d-don't think I'd mind so much," said Jessy slowly, "if sh-she didn't ch-change her mind so often. It's like—it's like the tr-treasure hunters Curtis used to t-talk about. J-just wandering around w-waiting to f-fall over the tr-treasure, without using th-their heads to f-find the cl-clues where to look."

"I shouldn't say bad things about your mother since I never even met her, but how she could go off and leave you and Tad, break all her promises, and—I just plain don't know!" Marly cut herself off sharply and got up. "Want some bananas and milk? I'm going to have some."

"Ba-na-na! Ba-na-na!" said Goldie happily.

Jessy got out the milk. "Wh-what promise?" she asked.

"Marriage. Marriage is a promise to the person you marry, and to any kids you have." Marly cut up the bananas with quick motions of the knife.

"You l-left Matt's dad," said Jessy slowly.

"No, I didn't!" said Marly indignantly. "He left me! I tried for over a year to—oh, but that's all gone now. And I'm almost glad, because you and Tad—well, life is better now."

Jessy swallowed, watching Goldie gobble up her share of banana. "Wh-what if, if we hadn't found the tr-treasure, and you'd g-gotten an interior d-decorator job, and it would've paid the t-taxes, but not for all four of us to live, only you and Matt—w-would you have sold this pl-place and gone back to Wichita?"

"Of course," said Marly. "If there'd been no way around it."

"B-but you hate Wichita."

"Oh, dear. Did you hear me say that once? I never meant to run down your hometown, honey—but I did hate it. Not because there was anything wrong with it, really, but just because it wasn't San Antonio." She brought the bowls to the table. "Your dad and I had a big fight about that once. He wanted to go ahead and quit the school in Wichita, burn all our bridges behind us. He said it was time I got what I wanted in life, even if it meant taking risks, instead of sacrificing what I wanted for other folks, like I did with Matt's dad. It was hard to make him see that what I wanted in life was all of us to be together."

Jessy picked up her spoon, but didn't eat. The knot inside her that had been tight so long she'd forgotten to feel it, began to loosen. "So you wouldn't have d-divorced Daddy to live here?"

"Of course not!" Marly sounded appalled. "You never thought—that's not why you were so anxious to find the treasure, was it?" Jessy nodded. "Well, you put that idea right out of your head! If I'd known you were thinking that I'd've—I'd've—next time ever you think something that awful, you come straight to me or Tad! We can't have you worrying about things like that."

The knot untied completely, and Jessy smiled. "It's ok-kay now. Wh-where's Daddy?"

"He got a call to go substitute for a math teacher who sprained his ankle. He'll be along about the same time as Matt." Marly ate her bananas. Goldie finished hers, and croaked like a grackle. "What was your day like?" asked Marly.

Jessy wiped milk from her chin, and told her about Anjanette.

GLOSSARY

ad·a·mant (ad′ ə mənt) *adj.* Not giving up easily. *She is adamant about keeping her after-school job.*

ad·dle (ad′ əl) *v.* To make or to become confused. *The big words in the heavy book addle the students, but they keep on reading.*

ap·pall (ə pôl′) *v.* To cause to feel shock or be greatly upset. *She is appalled that no one reported the crime.*

be·tray (bē trā′) *v.* To give something away without meaning to. *He says he doesn't care, but his quivering mouth betrays his feelings.*

com·mune (käm′ yo͞on) *n.* A group of unrelated people living together, often with a leader, sharing their work and earnings. *The commune supports itself by growing and selling fruits and vegetables.*

crude (kro͞od) *adj.* Rough, clumsy, not carefully thought out. *It's obvious from their crude questions that they don't study, and they don't care about the subject.*

des·ti·tute (des′ tə to͞ot) *adj.* Having no money for living; very poor. *The man lost his job and couldn't find work for three years, so he was left destitute.*

en·deav·or (en dev′ ər) *n.* Effort or work. *They worked hard at the bake sale, and the endeavor paid off with big earnings.*

ex·cess (ek′ ses) *adj.* More than what is needed; extra. *After the banquet, the excess food was given away.*

fi·na·gle (fə nā′ gəl) *v.* To get something by being clever or tricky. *The girl tries to finagle extra points for her team, but the other players don't agree.*

ford (fôrd) *n.* A shallow place in a river where a person can walk across. *They carry the canoe over the ford and onto the island.*

fu·tile (fyo͞ot′ l) *adj.* Hopeless, useless, not capable of producing any result. *He made a futile attempt to give up desserts in order to lose weight.*

haugh·ti·ly (hôt′ ə lē) *adv.* Showing too much pride in oneself while looking down on others. *The vain boy walked haughtily down the street, not saying hello to anyone.*

in·ven·to·ry (in′ vən tôr ē) *n.* A complete list of goods and property. *The entire inventory of the store was on sale.*

mi·ser (mī′ zər) *n.* A greedy, stingy person who saves up money without ever spending it. *He puts every penny he gets into the bank, so his brother calls him a miser.*

ob·lit·er·ate (ə blit′ ə rāt) *v.* To wipe out, erase completely. *The rain will obliterate the child's chalk drawing on the sidewalk.*

pal·o verde (pal′ ō ver′ dā) *n.* A small plant or bush that has few leaves. *They planted a palo verde in their backyard.*

re·source (rē′ sôrs) *n.* Something that is available to take care of a need. *The bank is a resource for money when you want to buy a house.*

tan·trum (tan′ trəm) *n.* A fit of bad temper. *Everyone says she's immature because she's always having a tantrum.*

vi·sion (vizh′ ən) *n.* A dream of something wonderful for the future. *The great man has a vision that one day all people will be friends.*